# ONE DEAD LAWYER

# ONE DEAD LAWYER

***A David Price Mystery***

***Tony Lindsay***



**Q-Boro Books**
WWW.QBOROBOOKS.COM

An Urban Entertainment Company

Published by Q-Boro Books


ISBN-13: 978-1-933967-29-5
ISBN-10: 1-933967-29-3
LCCN: 2006935888

First Printing December 2007
Printed in the United States of America

10 9 8 7 6 5 4 3 2 1


Cover layout/design by Candace K. Cottrell
Cover photo by JLove Images; models Nathalie DuBois and Jevone Smith; Styling by Candace K. Cottrell; Makeup by Magali
Editors: Tee C. Royal, Camille Lofters, Candace K. Cottrell

Q-BORO BOOKS
Jamaica, Queens NY 11434
WWW.QBOROBOOKS.COM

For my daughters; Tiffany, Joy and Kimberly

Love you,
Daddy

# Prologue

I am not a man who often resorts to violence. The fact is, being African-American, six foot two and 250-pounds-plus, with a shaved head, I try to avoid the violent reaction because so many people expect it from African-American males. There are, however, situations when a brother does what a brother got to do. Attorney Randolph Peal and I had found ourselves in such a situation.

I was holding him with my left arm wrapped around his neck. My right hand held my .9mm pistol to his temple. I wanted to kill him because in my soul I was certain that he'd either had them killed or done it himself.

We were on the Persian rug that covered the floor area in front of his large leather-padded desk. I tightened my arm around his neck. Kneeling behind him I could see the bald spot on the top of his narrow head. Dandruff had formed around the roots of his remaining dishwater-blond hair. I moved the pistol from his temple to the bald spot.

I wanted to blow a hole in his head, to scatter his brains

across the fancy rug and buffed-wood floor. I wanted to see his blood splatter as theirs had. I wanted to end the shyster's life . . . but I didn't. Not because my desire for his death lessened, but because I was hit hard on my own head from behind.

# Chapter One

I come to, and the sun is shining bright into my eyes. The front seat of my best friend Ricky's Ford Expedition is where I am. Flipping the passenger visor down gives me relief from the intrusive afternoon sun. Ricky is sitting in the driver's seat and behind me is my ex-wife Regina. There is an egg-sized lump growing on the back of my head and Ricky's .38 pistol is the seat next to him.

The pistol is customarily under his shirt, so, seeing it out from under his black short-sleeved shirt, I summarize that he and it are responsible for the lump on my head. Ricky Brown is well over 350 pounds and at least six feet three inches tall. He doesn't do much to exert himself, so seeing him labor for breath has me wondering.

My guess is it's from carrying me out of the lawyer's office, and his heavy breathing confirms my speculations. Despite the painful throbbing, I notice the black, linen short suit Ricky is wearing is actually very sharp. I would wear it. But why he chose to wear it with a pair of dressy, baby-blue alligator shoes is beyond me.

Ricky's eyes are focused on the police squad cars in front of the lawyer's building. There are at least six.

We are parked in downtown Chicago across the street from the monstrously large city hall building on the corner of LaSalle and Randolph. The lawyer's office is in the high-rise on the far south corner. This side of the street is lined with high-rise buildings. Regina reaches over my shoulder and drops my .9mm in my lap. She doesn't say a word to me. Downtown shoppers and workers walk up and down LaSalle Street staring back at the squad cars. My own alertness is kicking in, and the squads have my attention as well.

"Are they here for me?" I ask.

"What da fuck do you think? Of course they here fo' yo ass. You cain't go up in no big-time lawyer's office and put a pistol to his head. What da fuck was you thinkin'? We agreed to a plan. Man, you got to stop thinkin' wid ya heart. Shit. We'll be lucky to get da hell away from down here." His words are directed to me, but his gaze remains on the squad cars and police officers piling out of them.

My buddy Ricky has a big head, a huge head. Last week we went to Bacon's hat shop on 47th Street and he was measured at an eight and a half. The hat maker and I shared a good laugh at his expense. To make matters worse, Ricky draws attention to three quarters of a watermelon-size head by continuing to wear his hair in a slicked-down process in a finger-wave pattern. A style that, in my opinion, was played out in the seventies, when he first started wearing it.

"Look-a-here, D: I'm too old fo' stupid shit. And goin' up in there was some stupid shit! We had his ass, lock, stock and barrel. All you had to do was follow da plan. Goin' up in there was just plain stupid!"

I have no reply. He is right. It was stupid, but there are

times when stupidity is satisfying, and having that shyster at the end of my .9mm was very satisfying. It was very satisfying indeed. Admittedly, seeing his eyes buck, feeling him tremble in my grasp, watching his urine spread down his pants leg and hearing him whimper for his life pleased me.

"Man, what is you grinnin' about?" Ricky sees my satisfied smile. "Dis situation ain't funny. You sick, ya sittin' here damn near laughin' and dem damn cops up da block lookin' fo' ya ass. I sho' wish you would tell me what's funny."

The good thing about good friends is you can communicate beyond spoken words. His words were harsh, but once Ricky sees the grin on my face, he too starts to grin. Without me saying a word he feels my satisfaction. His fat, round, tan-colored face gives way to a full, toothy smile.

"Man, I gots to know; was dat piss stainin' da leg of dat fine suit? Did you make dat man piss his pants, D? I gots to know."

Before I can answer Ricky, Regina cuts me off by announcing, "I'm calling him."

"What?" Ricky and I both ask, turning around in our seats to face her thin, bright, unsmiling face.

"I'm calling him. We need to let him know we have some leverage in case he is thinking of giving the police your name." Before either of us can object, she opens her tiny flip phone and dials his number. I rub the sore lump on the back of my skull. My whole head begins to throb harder.

This summer has been a hot one. Ricky has the air conditioner on maximum, but as I rest my head against the passenger window I can still feel the afternoon heat outside.

"Regina Price for Attorney Peal . . . I'm aware he is in a meeting, Veronica, but put me through anyway . . . Randolph, this is Regina. Yes, of course I'm fine. I have nothing to fear from David or his friend, but I cannot say the same for you. What I'm saying is that if you give David's name or description to the police they will act in accordance. Of course I'm not threatening you . . . It's not a matter of whose side I am on, it's a simple matter of you not turning him over to the authorities or pressing any type of charges . . . I am really not concerned with how this looks to you. Yes, things have changed . . . Dinner tonight? It's a possibility. Call me around eight. Goodbye."

Again I turn around to face her. I must not have heard her right. "Did you agree to dinner with that murdering bastard?"

"Yes, because I don't know that he killed anyone. That is your suspicion." She answers quickly, with her emerald eyes rolling away from my accusing gaze, then out the window. "And I also got him to agree to not give you over to the police, which is more to the point of our current situation."

Her two-piece business suit, a soft summer white, buttoned to the collar, goes well with the "stay out of my business" attitude she's offering me. The painful throbbing from the back of my head is increasing looking at the snide, "ain't nobody's business if I do" expression on her face. Her eyes roll back to me.

"I would expect a little more gratitude considering I just saved you from jail."

Although the street is filled with people, although the afternoon sun is beaming through the spaces between the thick high-rise buildings, and although Ricky is in the truck with us, in my mind, I am in a dark tunnel with Regina and the tiny cell phone she used to call that shyster.

I see my hand snatch it from her. The truck door opens, and I begin stomping the little phone into the concrete sidewalk. The downtown strollers scatter away from the spectacle of me demolishing every bit of her tiny gadget and stomping it to smithereens.

When I get back into the truck, Ricky is bent over his steering wheel laughing at my adolescent display of anger.

Regina remains cool in the backseat.

"That phone retailed for three hundred and seventy-five dollars. I expect payment in full."

I hear her, but I don't answer her. Al Sharpton will be wearing dreads and Whoopi Goldberg will be in a perm before I pay her a damn dime for that phone. The whole situation is her fault, hers and hers alone. And to think I really thought we had a chance of getting back together. I must have been trippin'.

"Ricky, drop me at my car, man. I'm in the indoor parking lot on Adams."

Sliding into my Cadillac DTS, I notice the date, Wednesday, August 13, 2003, on the small screen of my cell. The phone is in a hands-free mount attached under the dash. Tomorrow is my mother's birthday. Maybe I'll fly out to Arizona next week and surprise her and Daddy. I have been promising them a visit for over a year.

The DTS starts right up. This black-on-black-in-black sedan is by far the best Caddy I have ever owned. I traded both my Fleetwood Brougham and El Dog for it. All I want and need right now is one car. A brother is tired of maintaining two and three cars. Besides, even if I still had them, all I would drive would be this one. This Caddy rolls.

The kid loved it too. The kid . . . damn, I had been starting to like him again. Only a heartless, soulless person could kill a child, or a person so threatened they would forsake what's right for self-preservation. The latter I believe is the case with Attorney Randolph Peal, the man whose head I just had my pistol to.

He did kill them. I'd bet my right arm on it, and if Ricky hadn't stopped me I would have ended it. No more African American people dying at his hands. With Attorney Randolph Peal it's not a black/white thing; with him it is a green thing, an assets thing. He killed them to maintain his wealthy status, the sick bastard.

In the short time it takes me to exit the parking lot, the sedan has reached a comfortable seventy-two degrees and Miles's trumpet in "Green Haze" is trying hard to mellow me out. I rest my head easily against the headrest, conscious of the lump. It remains sore, but the throbbing is gone. The subtlety of the headrest's soft calf leather provides an almost therapeutic touch.

Pulling from the inside parking lot onto Adams Street, I stop to say a couple of quick thank-you prayers. First, I thank God for having Ricky stop me from killing the lawyer. I continue by thanking Him for not letting the police catch us coming out of the lawyer's office, and I thank Him again for my son.

During the last four months I have been getting acquainted with my four-year-old son, a child I hadn't known existed. Regina kept his birth and life a secret from me. It wasn't until she thought I was on my deathbed that she brought him to me.

Chester is our second son. Our first son, Eric, died due to an underdeveloped heart. A big piece of me died with him. I have never felt whole since his death. Chester has not nor ever will replace Eric, but he has brought me joy. When I first laid eyes on him from my hospital bed, my life got better. A warmth opened up inside my chest, and it has been growing ever since.

My boy, my son, is truly a gift from God. His smile, his bright eyes, his soft voice, each and every little nap on his tiny head gives me reason to thank the Lord. I love the child, and because of him once again I have a life worthy of living.

When I first got out of the hospital, Regina set no boundaries on me visiting my son. She opened the doors to the home that used to be ours. I could stop by to see Chester whenever. And since I am one of the principals in a personal security firm, our time together is often. I am there to pour the milk over his Froot Loops in the morning, and more times than not we close his Pooh Bear books together before bedtime. Things were going great between us until Regina dropped the bomb on me.

I should have seen it coming, but I didn't. I was too busy thinking Regina and I were going to be a family again. The three of us were doing family things: matinee shows, Chuck E. Cheese pizza, Lincoln Park Zoo and the Children's Museum. It was all good, or so a brother thought.

While it's true Regina and I never went anywhere alone, I was still certain it would only be a matter of time. My thinking was wrong. Three days ago, she called me over to her place at twelve-thirty at night. I thought, *it's the booty call a brother's been waiting for*. It was a booty call, all right, except I was the one who got stuck.

Man, this city is changing form right in front of my eyes. Every time I pull up to this intersection at Halsted and Roosevelt, I trip on how much the area has changed. Maxwell Street, for practical purposes, is gone. No more Polish-sausage stands, no street peddlers, no cheap sweat socks, no price-haggling retail stores, no head shops, no blues music flowing through the air, no corner-to-corner people-filled blocks, no knife-sharpener's wheel, no rag man, no fish carts, no five dollar "gold" chains, no ten dollar "Rolax" or "Monado" watches, no all-African-American-cast nasty videos, no more single-hubcap deals, no Three-Card Molly players, no fruit wagons, no more Sunday mornings on Maxwell Street; it's all gone. Barren, flat, fenced-in city lots are what remains. They say the area will be "urbane" once the building starts and is finished, but now, to me, it looks like a flattened community.

Maxwell Street used to be Sunday-afternoon blues, fresh fried fish, the flea market, cheap gym shoes, Dobbs hats, Stacy Adams shoes and Tino the Tailor. I bought three suits last year, and I still haven't found a place to take them to get altered. Tino has been hemming my pants since I was twelve years old. This part of the city no longer feels like the Chicago I grew up in. The cultural hot spot it was is no more.

Regina told me she has been talking about living north of here and told me I should think about relocating downtown. I told her it wasn't affordable for me. A brother can afford it, but I don't want any part of this so called re-gentrification. As far as I can see, all they are really doing is moving folks out who are not rich.

I make the left onto Halsted and go into an immediate U-turn. I make the right on Roosevelt. They moved the Polish-sausage stands to Union Street; the street that runs alongside of the Dan Ryan Expressway. The Polish-sausage stands have been converted into a couple of trailers, but the sausages are still good; smothered in grilled onions and topped with hot peppers.

I just got the Caddy detailed, but since Regina won't be riding in it anytime soon, the smell of the grilled Polish sausages and onions won't be offending anyone. I personally enjoy getting in my car a day later and still smelling the scent of the sandwich, but that's me.

Instantly when I get out of my Caddy the heat assaults me. The sun is beaming strong and the air is heavy. Extreme, that's Chicago weather, scorching in the summer and freezing in the winter. I break a twenty for two Polishes, fries and two cans of pop. I give the kids begging in front of the trailers all the change. I know giving them money only encourages them to beg more, but one of them might really be hungry. Better to help the one in need than none.

Back in the Caddy I've got the air blasting. A brother broke out in a sweat just that fast and wasn't out three minutes. Sitting in front of the trailer stand wolfing down my Polishes, I watch the four kids counting the change. They scream in happiness and run back to Roosevelt. The money must have made their day.

I need to be calling Carol, my business partner, to check in and explain to her what happened; however, that's not where my head is right now. Besides, she is surely going to want to talk about the murders, and my heart is not up to it.

I throw the fries out the window to the begging common snipes. For most of my life I called these large birds seagulls, but when I took Chester to the zoo last week I read on one of the plaques that they were named common snipes. You can learn something every day if you're looking.

I wash the Polish sausages down with two pops, stuff the empty cans in the brown paper sack my lunch came in and resist the temptation to throw it out the window. After all, it would only be adding to the litter all about the trailer stand. A UPS truck pulls alongside me and blocks my exit. It doesn't anger me because I'm in no hurry to correct my mistake. I shouldn't have gone to see Attorney Peal.

I screwed up Regina and Ricky's plan big–time, and since I was the one who aborted it, it's up to me to set it back in motion. My job was to motivate Randolph Peal's ex-wife into going to the police against her murdering ex-husband. I was to go see her, not him, but the murders got me to seeing red and I had to get with Peal. It's like Ricky said: I've got to stop thinking with my heart.

The UPS driver buys a sack of sandwiches. He walks in front of my Caddy and purposely avoids looking at me because he knows he had my car blocked in. With the truck gone I have a clear shot to the expressway's on ramp.

The small traffic light on the ramp stops me from merging immediately. This makes absolutely no sense to me. A traffic light on an expressway ramp—why stop a vehicle that needs to gain speed to merge? It's ludicrous. The flow of traffic is light heading south, and that's a good thing; it shouldn't take me more than forty minutes to get out to the attorney's ex-wife's estate.

This whole sad affair started out as a favor to Regina. It was her girlfriend Daphne's son I was supposed to keep safe. The young man was involved in much more than a threat from a gang selling crack cocaine, which is the lie he told his mama. In the beginning I thought it was a simple enough protection case, a middle-class kid trying to play thug who got in over his head and ran back home to his mama for safety. But I was wrong, dead wrong.

# Chapter Two

Three nights ago I was at home in a laid-back mode. It was muggy outside, but the central air had the place feeling crisp and the new housekeeping service had put fresh sheets on my high-post bed. I was apprehensive about getting a housekeeping service because it felt like I was frontin' or something, acting the part of a big shot, but a brother really needed some help, somebody to cook, wash and clean up, somebody who did it better than me. I could never really get the place clean like it was supposed to be. Sure I mopped the floors and washed the dishes, but the dishes stayed in the rack on the counter, and my oven and microwave were biohazard zones. I don't do household chores well.

About two months ago I was flipping through the newspaper and saw an ad for a household-management service. For a monthly fee, one that I now feel is way less than what I should pay for the services, they take care of everything. They vacuum, mop floors, clean windows, wash dishes, cook three good meals a week and do the laundry. I do, however, wash my own underwear, some things others shouldn't do for you.

They put out fresh towels in the bathroom and clean sheets on my bed. The service is great. I'm gone most mornings so I hardly ever see them working, which is cool because I still feel a little guilty about having people cleaning my house. However, when I enter my home, the place is neat and clean and I love it all the more. It's as clean as my grandmother used to keep it, which is how a house is supposed to look.

That night I was stretched out on my bed in a pair of Nike baggy shorts with two big pillows behind my back and *The Matrix* playing in my bedroom DVD player. I'd left Chester and Regina a couple of hours ago, but I was missing them. Mostly I was missing Regina.

Although we had spent a lot of time together, I had made no deliberate romantic advances toward her. My plan was to show her that I was ready to be the man she needed. Actions speak louder than words.

I started doing the tasks around her house that a husband would do: washing her car, cutting the grass, barbecuing, fixing the lose doorknobs, stopping running toilets, organizing the garage—and I paid a couple of her monthly bills while knowing full well the alimony the courts had me send covered most of her house expenses. I wanted her to get used to having me around again. I made myself available whenever she needed me.

During our small talk, we spoke around the past and never of the future. We conversed on the moment. We'd had a couple of innocent bumps and slight physical touches here and there, but nothing intentional on either of our behalfs until that afternoon.

On the way from the grocery store she held my hand on the drive to her house. And after dinner we were washing the dishes and while standing at the sink I had to wrap around her to reach up to the cabinet, she didn't withdraw when my body leaned into her. In a matter of seconds my jones was as hard as an old oak. When she felt my firmness she stepped away.

I hadn't been with a woman for over four months, and that had been of my own choosing. After messing up with Regina once, if there was any chance of us getting back together I didn't want to be the one at fault if it didn't happen. I wanted my desires to be centered on her and that plan of action was working for me because a brother wanted her bad. When the thought of sex entered my mind, I saw Regina. That night stretched out in my bed, I was thinking about Regina and sex.

My mind floated back to the times when we used to lay up and watch movies in the bedroom. We seldom finished watching a movie. Back then, our bodies couldn't lay next to each other without joining.

I was laying there remembering our healthy sexual life when her phone call came in. She said she needed to see me right then. I thought we were on the same accord because I sho' needed to see her right then as well. I slid into a white mesh T-shirt and some flip-flop sandals. All I grabbed were my car keys.

My plan was as soon as she opened the door I was going to get started: no words, only hot kisses and caresses. When she opened her front door, I got one hot kiss in before she pushed me back. For a second I felt her clinging to me. I felt her wanting me, but only for a second. Once she pushed me back her words let me know that I was the only one going down memory lane to our once-shared passion.

She was dressed in jeans and a white oxford shirt and it was buttoned to the collar. Out of my embrace, her demeanor was stern.

"David, I believe you misinterpreted my call."

She wasn't smiling. She wasn't teasing. She was informing me of a fact.

What was stiff on me subsided. This was not a booty call.

"I felt you were getting the wrong message from our time together. Please come into the living room and let's talk."

"The wrong message"—man, I was ready to leave and I guess my expression told her that because she added another "Please."

I followed behind her, watching her narrow hips in those tight jeans, thinking about how difficult it used to be for her to get out of them. She offered me a seat on the beige leather sofa I bought when we were married. She sat across from me in an armchair I'd never seen before.

The decor of the living room hadn't changed much from the time when we were a family. The tall gold lamps were the same, but the coffee and end tables along with the light gray carpet were different. While visiting with Chester, most of my time in the house was spent either in his room or the den.

Both lamps were on and the room was bright. It didn't feel like twelve-thirty at night, and I suddenly felt underdressed in my shorts, T-shirt and flip-flops. She scooped up a manila folder from the coffee table and began.

"David, we have both started new lives apart."

I didn't like the sound of her statement, but looking at her soft hair, combed back and hanging down on her long, slender neck, I ignored the tone and for a moment went down memory lane again. I used to love kissing her neck.

"It's never easy to start over, David, but we both have done it. We have actually done better apart than we did together. I would have never thought your protection business would have grown as successful as it is now. If we were together I believe my doubt would have hindered its growth."

I nodded my head in agreement. When we were married she wanted me to stay in mental health and go back to school and get a master's in counseling, even though I told her I hated the field. That was a constant argument between us.

"You have always been a trailblazer, David, following your own path, doing things your way and thinking your own way. My Lord, there is no way I would have agreed with rehabbing your grandmother's house, especially in *that* neighborhood. No, there was no way if we were together I would have gone for that. Englewood, my God, but Martha tells me it's beautiful though. And she tells me you and Ricky have been rehabbing houses out in Gary, Indiana too. Goodness, I thought that little African-American city was gone under, but I read they elected a white mayor years ago. So perhaps they might find direction."

We had been talking for just a minute and I sensed no good was going to come from this conversation. She was letting out the part of her personality I detested—the part that believed white people always did and knew better than our own people. When we were married, any tradesman or repairman who came to our house had to be white. This was another constant argument between us.

Regina was an African-American girl raised in the rich suburb of Glenco. Despite her best effort not to be, she was a bourgeoisie. When we were dating it was the part of her personality she talked about changing. She once told me her greatest fear was becoming like her mother. In her words, her mother was "a black woman who enjoyed the fact that her father's money kept her from being a common black woman."

Regina desired to be a regular sister in the struggle, one who worked to make ends meet. But she wasn't. Her folks had serious loot. Not that her mother ever gave us a dime when we were married, because she didn't. Marrying me put Regina in the day-to-day struggle she wanted to be part of. When we met, independence from her mother and her mother's money was important to her. She wanted to make it on her own.

Her mother made it clear that if she married me we weren't to expect any assistance from her. Which was funny to me, because coming from a black working-class family I didn't expect anybody to help us but us. Nor did I have an idea of what their help would consist of; had I understood wealth, I might have tried to work something out.

Regina's cousins who married in favor of their family's wishes received full stock portfolios, income property, employment offers from friends of the family, monthly trust-fund checks and financial advice from folks with money.

When we got married I figured our degrees and our desire to succeed would be all we needed. I was right, but the money wouldn't have hurt us one bit. Where we were working to get were her cousins' starting points. When we were worried about getting approved for an apartment, they were applying for a mortgage. When we were starting a joint checking account, they were diversifying. I had no idea how far behind her pack we were and if she knew she never spoke of it to me.

"David, I have sold this house and put a down payment on one of the new homes being built on Clark Street. We will be able to move in in less than a month." She paused and looked at me with concern I hadn't seen in her eyes in years. "I truly hope you are not too upset about this. As you know, the house was mine through the divorce, and I have the right to do with it as I see fit."

I said nothing, letting her continue.

"Mother's lawyers assured me it was all legal and my pastor assured me that I wasn't doing you a disservice by using the home this way."

"Your pastor? You're kidding right?" It came out with more of a sarcastic overtone than I intended. At the end of our tattered marriage I caught Regina in a hotel with her/our pastor.

She rolled her emerald eyes at me and said, "I changed churches, David. The man I was with in the hotel is no longer my spiritual advisor."

"I'm glad."

At that point two emotions were colliding in my head, anger and disappointment: anger from her past cheating and disappointment over the fact that it wasn't a booty call that had me in her house.

"Shall we return to the topic at hand?" She brushed aside her infidelity so easily she might have been discussing a knitting technique. "Selling this house freed up so much capital, David, and with a little help from Mother, I was able to secure the loan at a very low rate. You have to understand, David, next year Chester will be starting preschool and the nanny service Mother recommended doesn't travel this far south.

"Living in a better-populated area will benefit him greatly. You couldn't have thought I was going to continue to raise him in Harvey? Why just last week they arrested two boys on the corner for selling some type of drug. I don't want my son exposed to dangers I can prevent. Say something, David."

Say something? As far as the house went, I had put it

out of my mind after the divorce; it was hers. Rationally, I wasn't upset by anything she had said so far. A better area, a better school, all this was good for my son.

Then the thought entered my mind that maybe her plan was for "us" to move downtown. She mentioned me moving downtown before; perhaps she was testing the waters. I might have been able to stomach living in the loop if I had my family back in place. I began to feel hopeful; the anger and disappointment went away.

"Regina, I see nothing wrong with your plans. Of course I'm a little surprised, but I understand your concerns. You want the best for Chester, and so do I."

Her face relaxed, and she smiled.

"Yes, I do want what's best for Chester. David, are you seeing anyone? Someone special, I mean."

At that point I was certain the conversation had turned my way.

"No, baby, after I got out of the hospital I spent most of my free time here with you and Chester."

Between work and her and Chester, how could I be seeing someone? She had to know that.

"Yes, I thought that was the case, and I knew I was being slightly dishonest by not telling you that I am seeing someone. Someone special, I mean."

I heard her with my ears, but it didn't register in my brain. She couldn't have said she was seeing someone, someone special. Who, how, and when? Did he sneak over after I left?

"I didn't tell him until yesterday about our time together. Oh God, I don't know what I was thinking. Part of me was trapped in thoughts of perhaps there was a chance at an 'us,' but there is far too much water under that bridge."

I was confused—no, dazed. It didn't sound like she had

plans for me moving downtown with her and Chester. She was laying her cards on the table. I scooted up on the edge of the couch, trying to lessen the space between us.

"Regina, baby, I was thinking, no hoping that . . ."

"No!" She quickly yelled and closed her eyes for a moment. She sat further back in her chair. When she opened her eyes she said, "Let me finish before you speak." She took a long, deep, runner's breath and blew the air out slow. I taught her how to do that when we used to run together. Breathing the right way helps with stress and Regina is a person who seldom vents, so learning how to take the cleansing breaths helped her a lot.

"I felt I owed you, David, because I kept Chester a secret from you. You missed so much of his life because of my own confused emotions. I didn't want you back in my life due to a child. I wanted you to want me and me alone, but it never happened.

"Do you know you didn't call me once after your grandmother's funeral? True we were separated, but David, we made love that night. And you couldn't pick up the phone to call and say 'How are you.' I was your wife for eight years!"

My grandmother died shortly after our son Eric did. She was very dear to me and the two losses shut me down for a while. I was numb at my grandmother's funeral, and that night Regina and I went to a hotel as a couple even though we were living separated at the time.

"Regina I . . ."

"Allow me to finish, David. I think I have earned the right to tell you how I feel and felt without interruption."

Basically she told me to shut up. The rigid way she looked at me made it clear that she was certain she'd earned the right to be heard.

"We had a life, a family. Did you think our getting together that night was just a casual occurrence? I waited for your call for weeks. God, I thought you wanted me back in your life, but you didn't. Did you? It was just sex to you. Men! Oh my sweet Lord, you tore my heart out.

"I thought our making love that night was you forgiving me. I thought you were forgiving me, for my infidelity, forgiving me for our son's death.

"I missed that doctor's appointment. Me! I chose not to take him to the doctor that morning and that night he died. He died. Our son died because I didn't take him to the doctor. I know you blamed me. I blamed me. I blamed me!"

I went from the sofa to her. I wanted to hold her and tell her to let it go, to tell her I had forgiven her because it wasn't her fault, but she pushed me away. She pushed me away hard.

"Don't! Please go back to your seat."

She wasn't crying. Her eyes were cold and dry.

"I don't need your hugs now. When I needed them you gave them to whores."

I dropped to the sofa speechless. Wasn't a thing I could say; she was right. When we should have been together I ran to the streets. I didn't think about her needs. I thought about only stopping my own pain.

"Last night, Randolph asked me to marry him, and I accepted."

"Randolph?" I didn't know any Randolph who she would be dating, but she made him sound as common as salt. "The Uncle Randolph Chester's been talking about?"

"Yes he is quite fond of Randolph. They enjoy each other's company and Randolph loves Chester as if he was his own son."

At that moment a dunce cap could have appeared on my head and I wouldn't have minded one bit. Regina has an uncle named Randolph. I was thinking it was the same dude. I had no idea Uncle Randolph was Regina's new man, but it made sense; "Uncle Randolph took Mommy to the movies," "Uncle Randolph and Mommy bought me some new gym shoes."

"I thought Chester was talking about your Uncle Randolph."

"I figured you did."

She *figured* I did but didn't bother to correct me? This woman was one of a kind. With that statement, the past four months evaporated from my consciousness. I had created a false Regina as the object of my desire. In my erroneous thoughts, Regina wanted me as she did early in our marriage. I thought of her as the girl I dated, a sparkling smile and a person who looked to me to change her life.

However, the true Regina was sitting before me: the Regina I had hurt, the Regina I caught in the hotel with the preacher, the Regina who didn't take my son to the doctor on the day of his death. I didn't want that Regina.

"Well what can I say, baby? I'm happy for you."

Yep, I was about as happy as a crackhead in Utah.

"Are you really, David?"

Hell naw! I wasn't happy for her. I went over there thinking I was going to get me some. But not only was I being denied a little trim that night, it had become painfully obvious that she hadn't really desired me at all. I was the only one lusting.

"Yeah, baby, if this nigga floats your boat, I'm not going to be the one to sink it." And I really meant that. No matter how disappointed I felt at the time. Regina was right; we had too many issues as a couple to be together.

I don't think I continued to blame her for Eric's death, but who knew what would surface if we were together every day? And even though I wanted her body, I really didn't want all of her, her attitudes and moods for example.

Rekindling our relationship would have been a lot of work and working on a relationship is for those young and in love. And being honest, I was neither.

"Randolph's not a nigga, David."

"Well you know what I'm saying. If this brother is making you happy, I will not be the one to spoil it."

"Randolph is not African-American, David. He's white."

"What?"

"He's white."

"Come again."

"Attorney Randolph Peal is a white man."

"Hold up. Not that dude on the commercial. Please, Regina, tell me you are not talking about that ambulance chaser from LaSalle Street." I stood up from the sofa. "He's a crook, baby. That bastard is as slimy as a fresh booger."

"David, please."

"He is, baby. He is as crooked as the letter S. Everybody in the hood knows that. The sucker doesn't pay his settlements on time, if he pays out at all. I know at least fifteen people waiting to get their money from his shady ass. He is not close to right, Gina."

"You're mistaken about him, David. I've seen those ghetto people in his office demanding payments on cases that haven't been settled. It's pathetic. He goes in his pocket to loan them money because they cannot wait for payment."

"Yeah he loans them money all right; at forty percent interest!"

Her eyes were on me, but she wasn't focused. I wasn't getting through. She was not hearing my words. I decided to try a different approach.

"You know you wouldn't be his first black wife. He was married to Eleanor Jackson."

"So?"

"I'm just saying; he may be one of them white men with a thing for black women."

"Eleanor and I are as different as night and day."

"That's my point. The only thing you both have in common is being black. How long have you been going out with him?"

"Long enough to gather that he is one of the most honest, caring men I have ever met."

"He's a personal-injury lawyer, Gina. Caring is not one of their attributes."

"You're not familiar with Randolph the way I am. Your interaction with him I'm sure has been slight and from a jaded perspective."

"True, I have never met him, but I know plenty of people who have. He makes his living off of our community. Black folks with health and auto insurance have gotten him rich."

She stood to face me with eyes piercing and looked as if she were really going to set me straight. She was defending the man with a vigor I hadn't seen from her in years.

"Tell me how, David? He sues stores, trucking companies, hospitals, liquor companies, and retail stores. He helps people, David. Your opinion is shortsighted," she huffed.

"If he's such a help, why is it mandatory for his clients to be employed with health insurance?"

"The intricacies of a law practice are beyond me and you weren't trained in law either. What? Did your bodyguard training include a law course?"

A smirk rested on her thin lips.

I am secure and happy with my career choice. I am a personal security professional. Others, however, treat my chosen profession as a pressure point or as a dent in my armor. My job is to provide protection for those who need it. I am a security escort and proud of it.

"You know what? I'm outta here. If you want to marry him, hey, I'm fine with it, but my son won't be anywhere close to him."

"He wants to adopt Chester."

"Hell naw! I know you didn't say what I think you said!" I stepped to her and she backed up as if she feared me. I stood where I was. My intentions were not to be a threat. I was stepping closer to hear her, because I couldn't have heard her right.

"He wants to adopt Chester," she said again.

"How is he going to adopt a boy who already has a father?"

"It's legal, David. When we marry, he can adopt Chester, giving him his name and making him an heir to his estate."

"You have lost your cotton-pickin' mind if you think I will give my son to any man walking this earth!"

"It will benefit Chester."

"You know what, Gina? It's really time for me to leave."

I turned away to leave.

To my back she said, "David, please don't fight this. You can still spend as much time with Chester as you like. It's a simple name change, a name change that will set him up for life."

I wanted to turn around and look at her eye to eye, but I didn't. I didn't trust myself not to hurt her. She was talking about a white man adopting my son. I had to get out of there.

"You know what, you can bend over for that crook if you want to, but you won't be offering him my son. I'll see you and that shyster in court."

"If you take that attitude, Randolph will start the proceedings before we are married. He said he is willing to fight for Chester. He has been in his life longer than you."

At that I turned around. This broad had balls. She flipped open the folder to show me some papers, I slapped it out of her hands and the papers scattered across the table.

"And whose fuckin' fault is that? You kept Chester a secret from me!"

She didn't have an answer. She stood there looking through me. Man, I was out of there quicker than a Michael Jackson dance skip. I needed major space between me and that . . . that . . . that . . . woman!

# Chapter Three

I was outside at my Caddy patting the pockets in my shorts for the keys. I didn't have them. The night air was heavy and hot, and sweat was dripping from my bald head down the back of my neck. My keys must have slid out of my pocket while I sat on the sofa. I patted my pockets again for my cell phone. I'd left it at home.

I looked down the dark block to the traffic on 159th Street and wondered about my chances of catching a cab at one-thirty in the morning in Harvey, Illinois.

Maybe I could get a gypsy cab, was my thought.

As I started walking, a gold baby Benz pulled alongside my DTS. At first glance I thought it was my business partner, Carol, but it wasn't.

"David is that you?" a female voice called from the small sedan. "Good, it is you. I came out here hoping Regina would be able to get in contact with you tonight. I need your help."

It was Regina's friend Daphne. As pissed as I was at Regina, all her friends, her mama, and her dead daddy could have kissed my ass. I acted as if I didn't see the car or hear a word she said. I turned and started my walk toward 159th Street.

Regina's front door suddenly swung open and she screamed for me.

"David! Chester is hurt!"

The alarm in her voice drew me up the porch stairs, past her and straight into the house. Chester was at the foot of the stairs crying, holding his foot; blood was seeping through his tiny fingers.

"Daddy, Daddy, my feet, my foots, my toooe!"

I lifted my son and gently pushed his small hand aside. He'd sliced his big toe open. The cut didn't look severe. I carried him to the kitchen and rinsed his foot in the sink. I covered his cheeks with kisses while the cold water cleared away the blood.

It didn't take two minutes for him to go from crying to laughing. The splashing cold water tickled his feet. Regina brought us a First Aid kit. A quick rinse of hydrogen peroxide, a dab of Vaseline, a Band-aid, and a kiss on all ten toes, and my little trooper was none the worse for wear.

I carried him up to his room and he told me all about a new Scooby-Doo movie he wanted us to buy and watch on Saturday. I told him we had a date, and tucked him in under his covers. He was sleep before I finished the good-night prayer with him. When I came downstairs from his bedroom Regina was standing at the front door.

"He was running after you. He woke up, heard your voice and wanted to tell you about a new tape he saw in the Wal-Mart sales paper. He stubbed his toe on the door. I tried to help him but he wouldn't let me touch it. He started screaming for you."

"The boy wanted his daddy, you can't blame him for that," I said looking hard into her eyes.

I walked into the living room to get my keys from the sofa and saw Daphne and her son. They were sitting on the sofa. My keys were on the coffee table atop the manila folder.

"David, I need to hire you." Daphne was looking at me, but I wasn't looking at her. "It's my son. D, he's in trouble with some rough boys."

She knew damn well that she wasn't friendly enough with me to be calling me D. She was reaching, so I figured she needed my help pretty bad. I grabbed my keys and sat in the armchair across from the two of them. Regina took the love seat across the room.

When Daphne's boy was about seven years old, I liked him a lot. He was a fat little fellow, but he was a rough-and-tumble kid through and through. They lived across the alley behind us, in her parents' house. I used to watch him play and scrap. The boy was constantly up a tree or under a porch, and he was always dirty, but it was the day's dirt from his play. Daphne started him out clean.

He would bring stuff to me to look at that he found; rocks, bones, old-time spinning tops, bolts, whatever struck his fancy. I even built him a treasure box for him to keep all his stuff in.

I have never known the whole story, but overnight Daphne was no longer a single mom trying to make ends meet while living in her parents' basement. Young Daphne bought a condo in Hyde Park and a Volvo. From what I heard, she was now living downtown. For a time, after she moved out of her parents' basement, she would still bring the boy around to the block parties and family barbecues.

However, the instant wealth changed her, and I guess she changed the boy. He came to a block party with toys and wouldn't let any of the other kids play with them. They were to only watch him play with them. Kids who have a little learn to share, and he was once a kid who had a little, so the other kids on the block expected him to share. He nor his mother agreed. A fight broke out between the children. Harsh words were exchanged between parents, and Daphne and her son never attended another block party or family event.

That night at Regina's, the first thing I noticed about the boy was that he was blunted. He couldn't have opened his eyes all the way if he was in a squad room full of cops. The marijuana had him feeling right nice. For no reason other than me being in a foul mood, I decided to mess with him.

"Hey, Stanley! How you been, young brother?"

My blurted-out "Hey Stanley" sat him erect as a light pole. He surveyed the room as if he'd just arrived. The kid's hair was braided in cornrows with jagged angles that resembled the letter V.

"Oh, hey there, Mr. Price, I been doin' awright. School is goin' great."

It was mid-August; no high-school students had returned to classes.

"I didn't ask you about school, boy. What, did you have to go to summer school?"

"No sir, not really, I just thought you asked."

"You got allergies or something? Why are your eyes so red? And what's all the white crap around your lips? Damn, I wouldn't lick them if I was you. That stuff looks toxic."

He stopped licking his lips and shot me what I believed he considered a tough look and said, "Yeah I think I do have allergies. I'm allergic to old men trippin'."

His mother quickly intervened. "Boy, watch your mouth! Mr. Price might be nice enough to help you."

The boy and his mama were almost dressed the same.

Each had on a terry cloth sweatsuit . His was a gold Sean John; I had a black one at home just like it. Daphne's was gold too, but it wasn't one of Puffy's.

She had the widest hair rollers under her flowered headscarf I had ever seen. They were about four inches in diameter. It only took eight to roll up her whole head.

"I don't need his help." His droopy red eyes traveled from me to his mama.

"Oh no?" she asked. "I can't help, and you won't go to the police. So who is supposed to stop those wannabe gangsters from hurting you?"

"I told you, Ma, just give me the money and it will all work out."

"Boy, I'm not paying any young hooligans five thousand dollars!"

"It's only money, Ma."

At that statement I laughed out loud but his mother's reply was priceless.

"It's only money! Boy, *my* money and the word 'only' don't go together."

I was tired and had heard enough. There was no fear or worry in the boy's face or in his words. The spoiled brat was playing his mother for money. I didn't have the patience for his games.

"If my help is not needed, I'm going home."

"See ya," the kid said and shot me a half grin.

That pissed me off. If he would have just sat there and let me leave I wouldn't have screwed up his little scam, because Daphne was Regina's friend, and all associated with Regina could have kissed my ass.

His mother kicked him hard in his shin and said, "Boy, shut your silly mouth." She looked like she wanted to slap him but thought better of it.

"David, I don't know what you can do to help if anything. I found some drugs in a sandwich bag in his room. I told him I flushed them down the toilet and now I find out he was given the drugs on consignment. Five thousand dollars is what he has to come up with."

"What? Five thousand dollars and you said the drugs were in a sandwich bag?" I shot the boy my own half grin. He looked away.

"Yes, in a sandwich bag."

"I don't know of any street drug that could fit into a sandwich bag and be worth five grand."

"That's because you too old to be up on thangs and you can't help. Ma this is . . ." The boy tried to stand, but Daphne's hand was in his stomach and she directed him back to the sofa.

I ignored his words and asked, "Was it pills?"

"No, it looks like pottery chips or something. Here." She pulled the sandwich bag from inside her blouse.

The boy's mouth dropped open and damn near hit the floor.

"Ma, you said you flushed it down the toilet."

"Boy, shut up."

It was crack cocaine, and not even an eighth of an ounce. I was right. The kid was scamming his own mama. I wanted to leave, go home and lick my Regina-inflicted wounds, and then find myself a good lawyer. I didn't want a new case, especially a case that would help one of Regina's friends, but at one time I'd liked the boy. I took the bag of cocaine from Daphne's hand.

"This isn't two hundred dollars worth of crack cocaine. Stanley is lying to you."

My brother, Robert, is addicted to crack. I know the dollar value of it by sight. I have bought him enough eight balls, one eighth of an ounce to know one when I see one. The question I asked myself was why.

Why would the boy lie to his mother? Daphne had always given him more than he needed, and despite his flip mouth, at one time I knew him to love his mama.

"That's not five thousand dollars worth of narcotics?"

"No. It's not two hundred dollars worth."

My answer was to her, but my eyes were on Stanley. He was looking down at his elf-like gym shoes. They were that new style of nylon gym shoe with the curved-up toes. I didn't like them. I looked from the shoes to his mother. If she thought better of hitting him this time, thinking didn't stop her.

She went upside the boy's head with tight little fists, beating him all about his head and shoulders. I didn't move. It was Regina who bolted across the room and pulled the mother off her son.

Out of breath, and with big rollers undone and scattered across the couch and coffee table, Daphne ordered me to get her son, "the hell out of my sight!" Again I didn't move. I was about to ask her where she wanted me to take him when she asked, "How much does your protection cost, David?"

"Don't worry baby, it won't cost you five grand." I said the words to Daphne, but my eyes were hard on Regina. I was trying to let her know this was a favor to her. She looked at me briefly and nodded her head.

It was just the two of us alone in my DTS. The young creep hadn't said a word and we'd traveled for over three miles. Trying to con his own mother out of money made the kid a creep in my mind, but as a young creep, he deserved some help.

I spent a lot of time with kids. I coach a softball team in the summer and I sponsor a bowling league in the winter, mostly for the kids on my block and the block behind me.

I don't presume to be completely up on everything they go through, because kids these days go through a lot.

However, a spoiled punk when I was a kid looks the same as the spoiled punks of today. They have everything new and the most expensive version of it. The long gold chain that hung around the skinny kid's neck could have fed a family of five for six months.

"So your mama buys your clothes?" There was no traffic on I-94, and I drove the powerful black sedan through the early morning as if the expressway belonged to me.

"She used to, but I buy all my stuff now."

"If you got enough money to dress like you dressing, why were you trying to beat your own mama out of five grand?"

He made a teeth sucking noise and said, "Man, I wasn't gonna beat her out of anything. I woulda gave her the money back in a couple of days." He reached in his pants pocket and pulled out a box of small cigars. From the box he pulled a blunt. "You mind if I light it up?"

"Hell yeah, I mind. Matter of fact, throw that shit out the window along with the box of cigars!"

"Can't do that one, dude. I won't strike it up, but I ain't thowing it away, it's a whole sack in here."

"Young man, we are two black men in a Cadillac and I'm speeding. I am prepared to deal with a speeding ticket if I have to, but I am not about to get caught in a drug case because of your ass. Either you throw it out or we are going to the police station."

Driving with weed in the car didn't bother me at all. What got my goat was that he pulled the blunt out in front of me as if I was somebody he could get high with. I was not about to be disrespected by a kid who I had shoes older than.

"You trippin'," he said, but threw the blunt and the box of cigars out the window.

"Are you selling crack cocaine?" I asked. The kid didn't look the type, but I wanted to know what I could expect. Despite the façade he offered, there was a softness about the kid that didn't say drug dealer.

"Hell naw! I just bought that so Mama could find it. I ain't no penny-ante-ass rock boy, old-timer, I got game for real."

I had to keep reminding myself that at one time I'd actually liked the kid. And I had to remind myself that to him, I was an old-timer, or an "old hat," as me and Ricky used to call the older men in our area. For a second I had to think back and remember how old the old hats were. They men were older than their mid-forties. They were retired men who sat around checker boards for the better part of the day. They could be seen scattered throughout the neighborhood in garages or in the shade of a mechanic's tree, but the largest group of old hats congregated under the trees behind the church parking lot. We called them old hats because of the beat-up brims they wore. Sweat stained bans, thin spots in the felt, worn satin trim that no longer shone, dented crowns, wavy brims, and absolutely no feathers. These hats, like their owners, had seen a lot of life, and it showed. No. I am not quite an old hat, but to the kid, I guess I might have been.

"Oh yeah, kid, is that right, you got some real game? Cool, I'm always interested in opportunities. Tell me about your thing."

"I got a white boy hustle and it is so so smooth. Matter of fact, I might be able to get your ride paid off and put a couple of grand in your pocket."

I tried not to look at the skinny big-shot-acting kid as if he'd lost his mind. I forced a smile on my face and said, "I own this car, young buck, and I keep a couple of stacks in my pocket, but tell me about your clever hustle anyway." The DTS was floating at ninety-five miles per hour.

"Game is to be sold not told, old-timer."

"True that, young brother. The game is cold but fair, so you might as well share with another soldier on the square. Youngster, you speakin' like your game is lock. What is it gonna hurt you to help me get off the block?"

"Old nigga, you ain't no solider, and you sho' ain't on the block. You're ridin' a DTS Caddy and sportin' pinky rangs and thangs. Niggas still be talking about you and your boy from back in the day. I tell people y'all my uncles, D and Ricky. Man, y'all legends around the way."

I felt his eyes on me, but I was pushing the Caddy hard and I couldn't look away from the road.

"What are you doing around the way?"

Coming around the bend at 103rd Street I noticed some traffic ahead so I slowed the DTS. If he had been truly down my way, finding out what he was involved in wouldn't be hard at all.

"I be over that way a lot."

"Why?"

"I know people from around there."

"Who?" If he told me this I had him.

"My girl lives on Elizabeth."

"What's her last name?" I kept my eyes straight ahead, looking through the windshield. Even an inexperienced kid could see anxiousness.

"Gardner."

"Her daddy name Mitchell?"

"Yeah."

I was talking with Mitch about three weeks ago and he was worried about his daughter dating some half-slick young punk from downtown. She was going into her last year of high school, and Mitch didn't want her head getting turned by a boy driving his mama's Benz. Mitch wasn't sure, but he heard rumors that the boy was involved in doing phony car accidents. I decided to push the envelope a little.

"So it's you. Man, I heard about you. You're the young boy hooking folks up with the car accidents."

Then I looked over at him. I had to see how he reacted to my accusation.

"What?" The boy's eyelids were fluttering faster than roach legs. "What did you say?"

"You heard me. You doing the rear-end jobs with the trucks."

"What?"

Oh man, I hoped he didn't play poker, at least not for money.

"The rear-end jobs, you know, when a driver, a professional driver causes a truck to rear-end the car he's driving. You know what I'm talking about don't you? Ain't you the boy from downtown folks been talking about? Is that your 'smooth' hustle?"

He said nothing. It was his turn to look out the front windshield.

"That shit is not new, boy. The only thing new is you and your friends wrecking your parents' cars and driving up their insurance rates. Tell me, smart boy, are you getting paid from both ends? Your friends and the lawyer?"

"Ain't nobody said that's what I'm doing."

"You're only getting paid from the lawyer, huh?"

"I-I-I gets mine."

"Yeah, I bet you do. So why do you have to pay somebody five grand? What went wrong?"

I needed to know who the lawyer was, but I didn't want Stanley to know what I needed.

"Ain't nothing go wrong."

"Come on now, tell me what happened. I know most of it already."

When he turned and looked at me, I could tell he wanted to tell me everything. The boy was burdened and tired of the load. He needed help. For that brief moment I saw the little rough and tumble boy who played under my porch. I exited the expressway on 79th Street, taking the long way home.

"This dude wanted in; told me he had a job with insurance and car insurance. So I set it up. Turns out dude didn't have a job or insurance. The lawyer walked away from the case. Dude got pissed and he's holding me responsible for his ride being wrecked. I got about seven grand coming from the lawyer in a week from a couple of accidents I was in. I was going to pay for dude's car then.

"But dude got tired of waiting for me to fix his ride and sent those boys to my mama's house. She don't even let our cousins come to our new downtown place, so you know she flipped when she saw dude's crew sitting six-deep in a wrecked Olds Ninety-Eight in front of our house.

"She found the crack yesterday, so I figured it would all work out. I wanted her to be scared and think I was in trouble with some crack-selling gangster. She believed my lie and all, but dude's crew scared her and she thought about you."

"Oh, what a tangled web we weave . . ."

"What?"

"Nothing, kid. I guess your smooth-ass game ain't that smooth."

"Yeah, well, whatever. Can you help me, Mr. Price?"

The kid was asking, really asking, so he got my help.

"Yeah I can help you, Stanley, but it's going to cost you."

"How much?"

"Not money, young player. Your mama is going to cover my fee. From you I'm going to want hard labor, house chores." I smiled at him, but he was looking out the window, worried. "Oh, and by the way, what lawyer does the cases?"

"It be different lawyers, but they all work for the same firm Mama and her boyfriend work for, the one that be on TV."

# Chapter Four

By the time I got Stanley to my place Monday night, I was tired and annoyed. My mind was elsewhere. Babysitting a sixteen-year-old wannabe thug was the last thing I was in the mood for. I needed to get focused and call a lawyer to find out if what Regina and the shyster were trying was even legal.

It couldn't be. There is no way in hell one man could legally take another man's child. Not in this day and age. I began to worry over the fact that I had never seen Chester's birth certificate. Was I even listed as his father? And the bigger fear was, what if Chester really wasn't mine? Did Regina have some other proof? I regretted not looking at the papers she tried to give me.

"Hey, man, what the hell is this? The Batcave or something? Cut on the lights!"

If Stanley hadn't spoken, I probably would have sat in my underground garage for several more minutes. Involved in my own thoughts, I'd ignored the boy. I usually tell people about the underground garage before I pull into it. It can be a startling experience. I pull straight in from the street.

To the passenger it appears I'm going to crash into my house. However, under the porch is a garage door that opens in response to a recognition chip installed in the DTS. Once the car is in, the door closes and the garage is pitch black until I give the verbal command for lights. Sitting in the complete darkness with me not talking must have spooked Stanley.

"Lights please, Wilma" was the command for lights. The garage lit up completely. I said nothing to Stanley. My mood didn't allow for explaining the garage or the technology in it. The boy followed me in silence. Once we entered the house, Yin and Yang, my Dobermans, greeted us at the door.

They separated me from Stanley as they were trained to do. They held him at bay against the door. I introduced a petrified Stanley by giving the command "Friend," and they allowed him to pass.

"Wicked," was his response. "Man, this is some Fort Knox type shit."

Yin and Yang scared people. No matter how much money I offered the cleaning service, the owner would not agree to have her people feed them. They are trained to my voice command and also a sequence of chimes I have installed in my home-security system. I gave the cleaning service the code, allowing them to enter. However, it appears that in my absence Yin and Yang split up and follow the cleaning crew through the house while they do their duties. This apparently makes some of them nervous, and more times than the owner of the cleaning service likes, she has to come to my place and clean.

I showed Stanley to the guest bath and bedroom which was on the main level. As a result of remodeling, my home had been transformed into a two-bedroom house, with the master suite upstairs. Stanley didn't appear happy about being downstairs alone. I told him Yin and Yang slept at my door, but that didn't appear to settle him any. I told him there was a phone in the guest room and he could feel free to call his mother. With that, he settled in. I gave the kid some towels and a fresh bar of soap and headed upstairs.

I took off my mesh T-shirt and flip-flops and plummeted into the middle of my bed. The night had not turned out like I planned. I started thinking about lawyers I could call. A couple owed me favors, but I wanted a good lawyer, one with as many powerful connections as Randolph Peal. My oldest brother, Charlie, the Republican alderman, would have the associations I required. With that thought I was able to drift off to an almost restful sleep, until the phone rang.

Being in the protection business I often get calls at three AM, but an early-morning call is still an interruption. I yanked the phone up. "Yeah."

"D, it's me, Nelson."

"Who?"

"*Daaaphna*, from Harvey. A few hours ago we were over Gina's together. Remember? Those boys who were bothering my son are parked in front of my home. I was afraid to go in. I didn't want to call the *pooolice*, 'cause I don't know what Stanley's true association with them is. So I called Gina and she gave me *your* address. I'm parked outside your home. Is that okay? What should I do?"

She sounded a bit tipsy to me. I wanted to tell her to take her drunk behind back over to Regina's.

"Hold on. I'll be right down."

I was expecting to go outside, sit in her car and give some rational advice, but as soon as I opened the front door she was standing there and immediately got in my face. She was crying and babbling at the same time.

"I don't know what to do about all this mess. It's too much for me. It's way too much, it's all wrong and I know it. It's been wrong for a long time."

She fell against my chest, blubbering like a baby. Yin and Yang were at my side. They didn't try to separate us. They didn't even wait for the "friend" command, they just walked away and left me there holding her crying, reeking-of-liquor behind.

"I don't know where or who to turn to, D. It's all a mess, a mess I made and now my boy is in it. My baby involved in my shit, my shit, D."

Drunk or not, she was crying and obviously upset so I pulled her close, closed the door and walked into my living area. I sat on the couch and allowed her to sob on my chest. I was still half 'sleep when I went to the door and didn't think to put on a T-shirt. She didn't seem to mind crying on my bare skin.

Through continued sobs, whimpers and cries, she managed to put a sentence or two together.

"It has always been about money with me, D. Always trying to get more and keep what I have. You know my story. Neighborhood drunk for a father, got pregnant and lived in my parents' basement."

I'd forgotten about her father. He was the initial reason I began spending time with Stanley. He was so drunk so often that he couldn't play with the boy. I'd see him trying to do things with the kid, but he would either pass out in the yard or give up and stumble on in the house, leaving the kid standing there with a ball or toy in his hand. I started calling the kid over in my yard and we threw the ball around or whatever.

"The neighborhood pretty boy got me and four other girls pregnant the same year. Now I hear he's living in San Francisco being gay. Gay! How the hell you gonna get five girls pregnant in one summer and be gay?" She looked to me with dazed, unfocused eyes as if she expected an answer, but the crying took over again.

"I try so hard to do the right thing, but doing the right thing don't pay shit, not a damn thing. I would still be in my mama's basement doing the right thing. Seven dollars and twenty-five cent an hour wouldn't feed and clothe a baby and me. I wasn't wrong for wanting more. I wasn't, but it wasn't supposed to be like this, not like this, D."

One of her big rollers almost poked me in the eye. I tried to adjust her head while she sobbed.

"My baby wasn't supposed to be involved in my mess, he wasn't. Tonight my man, the same man who won't help my son, told me things were getting beyond his scope of control and that I should find counsel outside of him. Bastard!"

She dug her nails in my shoulder and really boo-hooed. I tried to move free of her grasp, but she grabbed hold of one of my pecs.

"The pain, it's all inside of me. I want it to stop. Oh God, make it stop. Gina said you used to take her pain away." Again her unfocused eyes were on me. Her whole face had drooped. "Help me, D. Make me right, make me feel right. Get this pain out of me, rod it out of me. Gina said . . ." Her hand fell to my lap and she gripped my jones. "She said you was big enough to . . ."

That was the last understandable thing she said. She mumbled, sobbed, then passed out.

I rose from the coach and got a sheet from the linen closet, took off her house shoes, stretched her out, covered her up and went back upstairs. That made it official; the past twelve hours had been whack.

When I got up to my bedroom, I dialed Regina's number.

"Heellloooo?"

She was drunk too. I hung up the phone.

Later that morning, I woke to the smell of frying bacon, brewing coffee and buttered something. I don't know if it was buttered toast, buttered English muffins or fried eggs cooked in butter, but I smelled butter and it got me out of the bed, in the tub and through the shower in record time.

I enjoy, no, I love having breakfast cooked for me. There are few feelings better than waking up hungry and having hot food waiting for you. I paused after I jumped into my shorts, T-shirt and flip-flops and thought about a life lesson. In the past, good feelings have cost. I pushed the negative thought aside and followed my nose to the food.

There on my grandmama's kitchen table was one of my grandmama's breakfasts: a saucepan full of bubbling grits with melting butter, a platter overflowing with bacon, a bowl of cubed cantaloupe, a stack of oven-broiled toast with butter, a bowl of scrambled eggs with melted cheese, and a big full pitcher of red Kool-Aid. Damn, if I wasn't grinning.

Seeing Stanley sitting in my chair stuffing his face didn't even lessen my joy. His mama was standing next to my new, chrome, double-sided, ice-making refrigerator smiling. She remained dressed in the same gold sweatsuit, but she'd undone her big rollers and her hair was hanging down around her shoulders. She must have taken off her underclothes, because I could see the imprint of her thick nipples and areolas. The night before I hadn't noticed, but Daphne had gotten kind of top-heavy over the years, adding curves to her slim, petite build.

Looking at her reminded me of a phrase Ricky used to tease thin women. In our younger, partying days, Ricky would walk up to a thin sister at a club and ask, "Tell me, sister, how long have you been afflicted by it?" Of course the sister would ask "what?" and he'd answer with, "The disease noassatall, does it run in your family or what?" He'd offer mock concern and even buy her a drink. "I hear that if you eat a little something it might help. Noassatall is nothing to play with."

Some women would get it and laugh along with us. Others would just accept the free drink and his pseudo concern, not realizing that there was no disease called noassatall only that they had no ass at all.

"I hope you don't mind, D, but I'm diabetic, so I have to eat when I get hungry."

I didn't think that food was on a diabetic's diet, but I wasn't asking.

"No problem, Daphne, as long as there's enough for me."

"Hush, you know good and well it's enough food for all of us. Grab a chair and dig in."

She had set the table for three, two at one end, one on the other. Stanley was sitting at the lone plate. I sat down, scooped up and grabbed some of everything, said a quick grace and dug in.

Daphne chuckled.

"What?" I asked between swallows.

"Nothing, it's just been so long since I've seen a man say grace, that's all. It's nice to see."

Stanley hadn't said good morning, but I hadn't said a

thing to him either. After a couple more bites, I asked him, "How did you sleep, Stanley? That's an old mattress in that room. I wasn't sure how it would work out."

The boy looked different by the morning light, more clean-cut. If it wasn't for the long chain hanging around his neck, he would have looked kind of preppy with his close haircut and clear skin.

"It was fine, Mr. Price. Everything was good. I let your dogs out in the back yard this morning. Was that okay?"

"Not a problem, young man. Thanks for doing it."

Daphne sat in the chair next to me. All she put on her plate was cantaloupe cubes, toast and grits. When she sat down she rested her hand on my thigh. I tensed a little but didn't stop eating. The food was good. It tasted like she'd sprinkled a little onion powder or something in the eggs.

"D, I want to thank you again for taking the time to work this out for us." She patted my thigh as she spoke. "I realize you are a busy man."

"What you are asking me to do is my business; no 'thank you' is required. This is what I do." No, it wasn't onion powder, it was garlic salt.

"Still, thank you." She smiled.

And then she squeezed my thigh and let her hand fall to the inside of it. Her hand was less than a quarter of an inch away from my jones. I had held myself for Regina close to four months. I was not a man to be played with. I told myself that if Daphne kept that up I was going to take her upstairs to get something I needed very badly. *She'd better leave me alone*, I told myself, but I didn't say a thing to her. I checked to see if the boy could see her hand under the table; he couldn't.

"Mr. Price, do you know what I thought about this morning?"

"Uh-uh, Stanley. Tell me."

I had a mouth full of grits and a fork full of eggs waiting to go in, and to my surprise Daphne's hand had gone under my shorts. She was maneuvering for a hand full on my jones. I flinched, but I didn't get out of the chair.

There was no doubt in my mind about the inappropriateness of what was going on. Daphne was Regina's friend. Regina was my ex-wife. Her friend's hand should not have been on my jones, but I did nothing to correct the inappropriate behavior because four months was a long time without the needed touch of a woman.

"That little treasure chest you made me when I was a shorty. You know I still got it. I use it for a jewelry box."

"You kidding me, Stanley, you still got that box?"

She was stroking me now and her touch was ever so soft. My jones responded respectively but I didn't stop eating. When I looked over at her she nodded her head yes and smiled.

"Yes sir, I do, but like I said, I don't keep nails and bones and stuff in it now. Mostly I use it for my gold and silver chains."

"You wear a lot of chains?"

"Well, you know I got a little bling bling," he said, grinning. A portion of last night's wannabe thug was starting to show.

"I don't wear chains anymore, Stanley. Would you like to know why?"

"Sure." He humped his shoulders slightly.

I put the fork down, drained my glass of red Kool-Aid and began. "I had a dream—no it wasn't a dream, it was more like a thought. I wondered what our slave ancestors would think if they came back and saw so many African-American people in chains. Would they think we were still burdened? Would they think that the white man still has us bound? Would they understand that the chains they died to have removed, we choose to wear? How could I explain to an ancestor that might have died in chains that I wanted a chain around my neck? Our ancestors chopped off limbs not to be chained. I don't even chain down my dogs, but I was wearing a chain around my neck. Think about that, young brother. I did."

Daphne's hand went from my jones to the gold chain around her neck. Now that wasn't my intention when I decided to spread a little knowledge. I was trying to put some fat on the boy's head, not stop his mama's hand from playing with my other head.

"That's deep, D. I never thought about my chains that way."

I picked my fork up and went back to eating. Without really planning to I nudged Daphne's thigh with mine.

She giggled and said, "You are full of surprises. We are really going to have to get to know one another. I would have never guessed you where such a conscious brother."

I don't believe sharing one thought qualified me as a conscious bother, but I do enjoy sharing my revelations. She placed her hand back on my jones and I was pleased.

"Mr. Price, I try to run a couple of miles every morning. I don't know if you know it, but I'm an all-state distance runner." He looked to me to see if I approved. I beamed him a smile.

"I've been running on a team since sixth grade. I kinda want to go for a run this morning, but . . . um you know . . . I ain't never been down this way without a ride. I mean I know a couple of guys, but just to be out running, I don't know . . . what do you think?"

"Are you asking me if it's safe for you to go running?"

"It ain't like I'm scared or nothing. I just don't know."

He was a wannabe gangster the night before, but by the morning light he was a cautious state runner.

"Yes, Stanley, it would be fine to run. There is a park four blocks up. You'll see a lot of folks out running. I suggest you leave that long chain, though. No sense in attracting attention. And go out the back door. It's closer to the park."

After talking to the boy the previous night, I figured he was in no real danger. The thugs wanted money to fix the car, not his death.

Stanley peeled off his Sean John jacket and long gold chain. He tightened up his elf-like gym shoes and left out the back door. It was just his mama and me. I looked at the stove clock. It read seven forty-five. My brother wasn't in the office, and I didn't know a lawyer who started work before nine. The time was there.

"D, last night over Regina's I watched you with Chester. I watched how you held and cared for your son." She reached under my shorts with no hesitation and grabbed hold. "It made me remember all the time you used to spend with Stanley and the rest of the kids on the block. But mostly I thought about the time you spent with my son, fixing his bikes, showing him how to fly a kite, teaching him how to swim. You're the one who got him into running track. Remember? He would try and jog with you on Saturday mornings." Gripping it, she moved her hand up and down its length.

"How I forgot all that I don't know, but it came back to me last night and made me want you. For the first time in years I was attracted to the man and not the man's money. I want you, D, in a country kind a way. Like my country grandmamma used to want my granddaddy.

"My grandmamma used to tell me it turned her on watching my granddaddy put a log on the fire, it turned her on watching him play with their kids, it turned her own watching him eat the food she cooked and it turned her on watching him put on a shirt she washed.

"When you walked in this kitchen grinning at the breakfast I fixed, you turned me on, when you covered me with that sheet last night, you turned me on, and when you said you would help my son, you turned me on. You turned me on in a country sort of way.

"I want you to hold me like we was in the country. Hold me like we was in a one-room shack with a busted screen door, on a slack board bed with a burlap sack mattress. I want to smell the fields and hear the chickens scratching. I want you to make me want some buttermilk and hot water cornbread. Send me to the country with this thang right here." She was pulling with one hand and caressing with the other.

"Last night me and Regina was drinking and she started talking. She told me how you thought she was calling you over for sex. I listened to her like a good friend should, but all the time I was thinking 'Lord, I wish he would have come over my house looking for some.'

"I told her I had to go home, but she kept pouring the wine and talking about the way, ohhh baby, the way you used to open her up, aaallll the way up inside. She made it sound so good. And I ain't been opened in so long. When I left my friend's house wild horses couldn't stop me from coming to you.

"I was drunk off her wine and a bit of my own cognac, and yes all the talking she did about you got me horny. I wanted you last night because I was drunk and horny. But I'm not drunk now, and I still want you."

That was all a brother could take. Regina bragged on me, but didn't want me, and there a woman sat who came to me because of what another woman said. I scooped her thin self up out of that chair and carried her upstairs to my California king–sized bed. When I got her to the bed I grabbed the top of her sweatpants and pulled them down while she was unzipping her jacket.

The sight of her breasts stunned me, and I sincerely hoped the image of them was forged in my mind forever. Remembering breasts like hers is one of the things that makes an old man smile while rocking away his last days on a porch.

"I bought these eighteen months ago," she said looking at me, "and a real man hasn't touched them yet."

They stood up like a porn star's. I reached for them but she moved out of my reach and lay back against one of my overstuffed feather pillows.

In my past experience big breasts were never perky and they hardly ever had long nipples attached. Slightly stuck and uncertain of whether to caress them, suck them or lay my head upon them, I allowed my open mouth to lead me.

Minutes later she whispered, "What you're doing feels good, D, but I'm in need something else. Right now, baby, I want you to bring the country on."

I wanted to bring it on. A brother was hard as a block of government cheese. I wasn't hesitating due to a lack of readiness. What was needed, however, was some calming time.

Premature ejaculation was knocking at my door. After four months with no sex, a brother could have easily gotten over stimulated. After I took a few deep, controlled breaths, I got between her open thighs. Soft, subtle resistance is what I found. It was easy enough to enter the head and a little more, but after that her warm softness encompassed me.

When I was a child, my grandmother would stew me apples, and with just the slightest push of my finger, the skin of the apple would open and my finger would be in the tender meat of the fruit. Sunken into the flesh of Daphne, I wanted to go deeper into delicateness so I pushed and pushed until I thought I heard her whimper.

I tried to pull back, but she grabbed hold of my butt and said, "No, no, don't you dare. Keep it there, slow and easy, D. Real slow, real easy, slow and easy, push it easy just like you doing." She pulled me into her.

After a while I realized it wasn't whimpering I heard. She was humming. She began rotating her hips beneath me and her humming got louder and her grip on my backside got tighter. The deeper I went, the more she rolled her hips. I wanted to pull out and stroke but she wouldn't allow me to retreat. When all I had to offer was in her, she stopped humming and locked her legs around the small of my back and humped. All I could do was stay in deep and that seemed to be all she wanted.

Beneath me I felt her quiver, What was tight and moist moments ago became slippery, wet and loose. The restraining grip that held my butt left. Her arms lay listless at her sides. Free to move, I did.

Her humming began again with my strokes, faint and barely audible, the looseness of her tightened. She dug nails into the top of my shoulders. I grunted in pain, but her humming wouldn't let it be heard.

Exactly what it was I don't know. Men call it, "hitting the back of it." Women refer to it as their "spot." With Daphne it was a patch of pleasure that I felt rising, no, more like swelling up inside her. When I repeatedly stroked over the rising mound and buried my head into what men call the back of it, she went electric. Her thighs wrapped around me tight and her nails peeled down my back and I became a "nasty, big-dick motherfucker."

I wanted to call her something too, but words escaped me as I too went electric. I didn't want any buttermilk and cornbread, but I sho' felt good. I thought I heard her say real quiet, almost under her breath, "sorry, Gina."

Sorry? I wasn't sorry. It was over between Regina and me. This brother was moving on, and I wanted to tell Daphne that, but the next sound I heard from her was snoring.

# Chapter Five

When I woke up, the clock on my night table read TUES 9:04 AM. I rolled free from our leg-tangled embrace, lifted the cordless from the cradle and dialed my office. Carol, my partner in the security service, answered on the first ring.

"Epsilon Security Escort Service, how may I help you?"

"Hey, Carol, it's me."

"Hey there, boss. Are you coming in today?"

I've tried for months to stop Carol from calling me that. We have been full partners for half a year and she continues to refer to me as "boss."

"Yep. I should be there within the hour. I need you to contact a divorce lawyer for me; a good one, one who is detailed and can go against a firm with political connections. Does anyone come to mind?"

"A couple. By the time you get here I'll have some choices for you. What's up?"

"I'll tell you later. Oh, and call my brother Charlie. Get some suggestions from him as well."

"Will do. Anything else?"

"Nope, that should do it. See you soon."

The morning activity Daphne and I shared put us both back to sleep. It had been a while since I came simultaneously with a woman. When it happens, in my opinion, two are truly equals. All pretenses are set aside when heartbeats match.

Sitting on the edge of the bed, looking over my shoulder at her I noticed she was awake and smiling. My eyes gravitated to her shaven pubic area, neat and inviting. Only a situation as significant as the threat of losing my son could have motivated me out of that bed. I bent to her and kissed a nipple, then rose from the bed. I had work to do. She sighed, pouted a little and sat up.

"D, I wasn't eavesdropping on your conversation, but I couldn't help but hear you need an attorney. I know one who may be able to help you. Interested?"

"Sure, baby. At this point I'm taking all the help I can get. Who are you talking about?" Her fingernail and toe polish matched, I liked that. The woman had a nice style about her. She scooted closer to me and started caressing my thighs while she talked.

"A friend, one who is familiar with how Peal operates."

"And how does he operate?"

I lowered my hand to her hair and played in it. Slices of sunlight beamed through the slits in the blinds. My jones was getting hard again because my mind went to her giving me some head. I was standing, and she was sitting, and her face was in my crotch area.

"Thorough and fast, and based on Regina's discussion last night she's trusting him to take care of it. What they are doing is wrong and I told her that last night. Something is going on with her, D. She hasn't been herself in a while.

The Regina I know would never think of taking your son away from you. Never."

I lowered my hand to the nape of her neck and played in her soft, thin hair.

"In her mind they are not taking him away from me. 'Just a simple name change' is what she told me."

I didn't want to talk about Regina's threat. I wanted to do something about it. Suddenly I felt as if I had been, and was, wasting time. The morning could have been spent laying out a plan of action rather than laying out Daphne. I pulled my hand away and walked from her stroking fingers toward the bathroom. Guilt is a motherfucker.

"The person you think can help, do you know them well enough to call this morning?"

"I can do better than that. I'll get us a meeting this morning." A smile rested on her face.

I offered her the shower first. She declined, saying her things were already set in the downstairs bathroom. I excused myself and headed for a quick shower.

Hiring Daphne's attorney wasn't a certainty in my mind. I needed information that would tell me if what Regina was threatening was legal. I decided to dress in a business suit. A charcoal gray, three-button pinstripe accompanied by a white shirt, light gray tie and baby-soft black Bally loafers.

Last month, my father sent me a custom-made holster from Arizona. It holds both my pistols right above the small of my back, and the loose way my suit jackets are cut makes my weapons undetectable to the untrained eye. On my right ankle I had a slender .22 harnessed. My pistols are part of my dressing; I seldom leave home without them.

As I was coming down the stairs, I heard voices in the back bedroom. Stanley's voice was familiar, but the female's was not. I hesitated at the first-floor bathroom and heard the shower running full blast. If Daphne was in there, who was in with Stanley? I walked up to the bedroom door and boldly pushed it open.

Hugged together, butt-naked in my childhood bed were Stanley and Mitch's daughter, May. Obviously frightened, May tried to roll behind Stanley and hide. He only grinned.

To me he said, "Man, D, don't you knock first?"

"What?"

"Ya heard me, partner! Ya supposed to knock on a closed door!"

The toothpick-thin irritant got out the bed and slammed *my* door, in *my* face.

"We be out in a minute; we wasn't finished. Didn't nobody disturb you and my mama! Why you come down here bustin' doors open? Old people be trippin'."

I was too taken aback to move. The slammed door froze me, but his words wrapped around me like duct tape. When anger finally freed me from my immobile state, I drew up my knee and readied to kick the door down until his mama, wrapped in a towel, jumped between my foot and the door. "Wait! Let me handle it, David, please."

"No. That's okay, I got this one."

I moved Daphne aside and opened the door just in time to see May scamper through the window with her blouse halfway down and shorts halfway zipped up.

To her fleeing back I said, "You better tell ya daddy before I do. You don't want him to hear my version!" She landed soundly on the wraparound back porch I had built in the spring. If the porch hadn't been there, she would have had to jump to the sidewalk. I stuck my head out the window and yelled. "I'm not playing, May. Tell your daddy something!"

There was no way I could tell Mitch I saw his daughter's half-naked ass climbing out of my window. However, I wanted to embarrass May enough to be afraid and feel a little shame, because my house is not to be mistaken for The Kiddy Motel.

The boy was standing there in his checkered boxers with an "I can't believe you just did that" look on his face.

"You shouldn't have barked at her like that. You got her all scared and crying. Man! She probably won't come back over. Damn! Why you do that?"

The kid really didn't have a clue. He didn't see a thing wrong with what he did, which made me turn my head to his mama. She avoided my look as she walked into the bedroom. A foot belonged up that boy's disrespectful behind. The thick skin of a leather belt should have met his hind parts. He needed a whipping. His mama should be going to the "country" on his backside, ripping off a tree switch and getting busy.

Deciding they needed some time alone, I was leaving the room until Daphne tightly grabbed hold of my hand and asked, "Will you stay David? I think we need to talk to him together. It was us he saw."

She was tripping; the terrible teen was hers, not mine. What he saw or heard was *his* mama getting *her* swerve on. It was a family incident.

I was intent on leaving until the kid said, "Ain't nothing to really talk about, Ma. We all adults here. I understand needs."

To that I answered, "Only two adults here, boy; that's me and your mama. You are a child, and you understand nothing of adult needs."

"I understand enough to know that both of y'all was knocked out, slobbering and snoring all over each other and that didn't happen because y'all got exhausted watching Oprah. Now did it? The trip is, y'all got y'alls and don't want me to get mines. Now what's up with that? From one playa to another playa, Mr. Price, is that right?"

I was about to tell the minor I wasn't a player, but his mother once again had the better words.

"Player! David is no player! To be a player he has to have played on someone. Do you feel he has played on me?"

Right before my eyes Stanley went from an arrogant, disrespectful young punk to a kid stuck between a rock and a hard place. His mother had him squirming in his stance.

"Ma, you trippin'. I ain't say that."

"You called him a player. That must make me what . . . the same as the young lady who just crawled out the window?"

"I ain't say that, Ma." His eyes were pleading for her understanding.

"What are you saying? No, what are you calling me? Me, your mother, what are you calling me?"

"Ma, I just said we all adults and I understand adult needs." He dropped his butt down to the bed. She stood over him with her index finger extended.

"What am I, the type of woman who needs something from a player? What did that young girl need from you?"

I could tell she was running all through his mind with combat boots on, smashing and mixing up emotions and thoughts. The boy didn't want to call his mama a "hottie."

"I asked you a question, boy. What did that narrow behind heifer want?"

"Nothing, Ma."

"She wanted something! She snuck her hot tail in here . . .

Lord have mercy . . . What is this I'm standing on? David, please tell me it's not one of those!"

It was a soiled condom. Her standing on it caused its contents to seep out and adhere to her foot. She lifted her foot to her son. "Pull this disgusting thing off me."

Stanley peeled it from his mother's foot. Then he jerked as if struck by an epiphany and asked, "What, y'all didn't use one?"

Touché for the kid. We hadn't, and I didn't even think about it. Our expressions must have told on us.

"Mama! You don't know him like that."

Oh, I could tell she wanted to hit him. She was trembling so I hard I thought the floorboards were vibrating. She wanted to hit him bad. Instead she ground her teeth, balled up her little fist, spun around and left. I had to bite down on the inside of my own jaw to stop from smiling in the boy's direction. Sternly, I told him, "Get dressed, boy. Me and your mama are going out. I got some work for you to do while we're gone."

He cocked his head and looked at me as if he wanted to say, "You ain't my daddy," but I cut him off at the pass with "And hurry up before I change my mind about helping you." True, I wasn't his daddy, but I was the man willing to help him.

# Chapter Six

Daphne wanted to stop at a lady's clothing boutique in Hyde Park before we went to see the lawyer she recommended. When she came out of the shop, the woman was dressed "shitty sharp," as Ricky says. That's when a person is dressed so well they develop a haughty or "shitty" attitude.

Daphne went into the boutique with slippers on her feet. She came out in a silver two-piece suit with a short skirt barely covering her business, white stockings and silver spiked heels. In the bold sun the silver shone like platinum.

Her suit matched my tie and her charcoal gray sunglasses matched my suit. I was grinning from ear to ear when she slid into the DTS. We were looking good. I love a woman who can dress.

"What are you grinning about, sir?" With her hair still on her shoulders, her prideful smile was bright and warm. She knew she was sharp as a razor.

"You baby."

"Baby? Mm, I like that, Mr. Price; feels like I moved up in status." The smile was seductive, and I moved to it. While I was kissing her soft lips, I pulled from the curve into traffic. "You looking mighty good there, Ms. Daphne." And that was the truth.

"Well, when you stepped into your top-shelf gear, did you think I was not going to do the same? I dress with a man. If you looking good baby, I'm going to be looking good right along with you; that's a part of togetherness a lot of people forget. It don't matter if we together for three days or three years, if we together, we should look good together.

"A couple makes a statement. If a woman is sharp and a brother is raggedy, what kind of message are they giving to the world? If two people are together they both supposed to be looking prosperous. If you got a black diamond mink, I want one too, and vice-versa. Couples make me mad not matching. We together, D, so our level of dress is going to be together. You're a sharp brother, and if I'm going to walk by your side I have to be proper." She leaned in and kissed me on my cheek, "Isn't that right?"

"You got it right, baby, and thanks too for helping me with this lawyer business. I mean the referral and all."

"You don't have to thank me for this. You are helping me save my son; it's only right that I help you save yours. We are together, D, at least in this. You and I against the odds, and I got to tell you it feels good having a strong back against mine, even if it is for only a short time." Her hand slid over my thigh to my lap. "Really good."

Daphne was putting the full-court press on a brother with all that togetherness talk, but I didn't mind. After the escapade with Regina, it felt good to be wanted. And being wanted by a smart, good-looking younger woman was a definite ego booster. I sat a little taller behind the wheel of my Caddy.

If Daphne and I were to kick it, the only stumbling block I saw was that hardheaded boy of hers. He would require patience. I looked over at Daphne's pretty, freshly made-up face and felt the cool confident demeanor she exuded, and then I thought about how tight, hot and wet her stuff was, and it didn't take me a second to decide that being bothered with the boy would be worth it. After all, I'd volunteered with kids. I had experience with today's youth. The kid wouldn't have been that bad. Stanley was like most teenagers; they want their opinions heard and valued.

"What were you and Stanley talking about out in the back yard?" Daphne had pulled her cell phone from her purse and was going though the menu.

"The deal he and I made last night involved him working for my help. I'm planning on expanding my vegetable garden next season. To do that, I need an area of grass cleared and dug up. I was showing him where to dig."

"And he agreed?" She sounded surprised. Her ears were listening to me, but her eyes were checking her text messages.

"Yep, he's going to expand my garden a bit, wash the first-floor windows and clean my grandmother's silverware."

"Well. You are going to have to tell me the exact words you used, because I have never got that much work out of him." She put the phone to her ear and began checking her voice mail.

"Your son is a challenge for you, huh?"

"D, challenge isn't the word. Please believe." She flipped the phone closed. The warm smile fled from her face when she spoke of her son. She wasn't angry, but her mood instantly became serious. "Stanley can take me there so quick. I have to pray to stop from killing him. I hear people say 'you spare the rod you spoil the child.' Lord knows I have beat my son, beat his ass good, but he still takes me there. It's almost as if he is trying to make me accept his nonsense. As if he's going to do what he wants to regardless of what I say.

"I swear if I didn't think military schools were full of racist, domineering, child-molesting bastards I would have sent him to one. I thought of sending him to be disciplined by his supposedly gay daddy, but that has never been a real option." She sucked her teeth and wiped nonexistent lint from her short skirt. "I suspect Stanley is entering the stage where he is changing from boy to man. That's why he thinks I'm stupid. A lot of men think women are stupid."

Her eyes cut over to me. I had no comment.

"He needs a man in his life. The truth be said, we both need a man in our lives." Again her eyes cut to me. "A real man, a take-charge, get-involved, decision-making man, a man who is not afraid of the responsibilities of family life. In my opinion men are supposed to lead, not offer options for consideration, which is what my current man does. I haven't had the best examples of men around Stanley. And that includes my father."

It became obvious that she wasn't going to stop talking and offer driving directions to the lawyer's office. Instinctively, I headed downtown.

"My current man is a boy himself, an infatuated boy. I didn't date with Stanley in mind, and I should have. I dated men who could help me financially, not thinking that these men were Stanley's male role models.

"Ninety-eight percent of the men I dated thought I was stupid because they were more financially adept than I. They all erroneously concluded that since I didn't know about managing money, I didn't know about managing life. I put up with their condescending attitudes to learn about money management, but Stanley witnessed me being subservient to them.

"It wasn't like they were calling me 'bitch' or slapping me around, but he did see me bow down. And I believe since he is coming into his manhood, he is expecting females to bow down and treat him in the skewed fashion he observed as a child. The budding boy wants to be a man, but he has the incorrect template.

"So yes, he is a challenge, but I am largely responsible for what he is, and I am not too proud to say that I need help in making him a man. I am trying to save my son too; save him from the male examples I provided."

She looked out the window as she spoke, I heard her voice calming and then something my grandmother used to say entered my mind.

"Daphne; there are no perfect children or parents. Raising kids is a hard thing to do. As my grandmother would tell my mother, 'Baby, after you raised some *chilrens*, ya have done somethin'."

Daphne didn't comment, but she did chuckle a little; either at my bad imitation of my grandmother or at the pigeon poop that suddenly splattered on the driver's side of the windshield. Two quick pushes on the wiper control, three wipes of the blades and the poop was gone. The DTS didn't play. It did everything to exactness. Traffic going toward the loop was light. We cruised all the way downtown.

"So who is the lawyer we're going to see?" We were coming up on downtown exits and I needed directions.

"We are going to see an associate of mine. Trust me on this, D. I won't steer you wrong. Please believe."

I had not been around Daphne enough to become familiar with what her expressions meant, but I would have bet a dollar to a doughnut that the way she sat up and the way her jaws locked meant baby girl was getting ready for a challenge.

"And you say this lawyer is familiar with how Regina's people do business?"

"Yes, very familiar." Her tone was not friendly. It was sharp and snippy.

"Exit on the Congress Parkway, David. You can go north on Dearborn then loop around to the parking garage on LaSalle."

Her whole persona changed once we were downtown. There was a military-like stiffness about her. A hardness was present. I said nothing; we were on her turf. A brother like me followed suit and put on my stone-hard game face.

While we were inside the parking garage the attendant directed us to a slot designated for monthly parks and didn't ask us for a dime. I thought it strange, but again she didn't comment, so neither did I.

I was cool with the hardcore demeanor while downtown. In my experience it proved best to be direct when dealing with folks in the loop. Directness is respected in Chicago. With stern face mode engaged, we were walking up LaSalle Street when Daphne threw me off. She grabbed a hold of my arm and snuggled up close to me. Her presence chased my hard exterior right away. I was back to smiling at her pretty face and finesse.

"Why you looking so mean, Mr. Price? Did I say something to offend you?"

"No, baby, you seem only capable of making me smile."

That got me a kiss on the cheek.

The office was located in one of Chicago's older, musty buildings. We stepped from the ancient elevator, directly into the firm of Peal, MacNard and Nelson. The name of the firm was above the receptionist desk in tacky gold plastic letters. My first thought was, *Damn, her lawyer must be broke.*

Standing at the receptionist desk, I looked down to Daphne who gave me a "don't you get it" look before she told the receptionist, "Veronica, have Martin meet us in conference room one."

The hint or point she thought I should have got, I didn't get. On the corner of the receptionist's desk was a message spindle, Daphne spun it to the slot labeled NELSON and took the message slips. She looked curiously back over her shoulder at me. I still hadn't gotten it. It wasn't until we walked past an office with D. NELSON scripted on the door did I start to get it.

"Oh! You are a lawyer."

A proud, youthful smile caused her eyes to sparkle. "Yes, for a little over six months." She was obviously happy about her accomplishment

"Wow! Color me surprised."

"I hope you like surprises, because I have a couple more for you." The childish smile turned devilish. Something more was brewing, I could tell because of the tingling in my armpits. Since childhood this tingling had been my early warning system.

"Not many people from my past know I practice law. I look ahead, not back. Here." She pushed opened two large doors. "Go in and have a seat, I'll be back in a second."

She led me into a standard meeting room. Where there should have been a long shiny cherrywood or slate table, there were instead three card tables pushed together, complete with vinyl folding chairs. Instead of prints in nice frames, there were motivational posters taped up with bits of masking tape; "Believe and achieve," "Expect the best" and "No I in team". The law firm's conference room looked more like a retail store's employee lunchroom.

Minutes later Daphne returned with a box full of office stuff, pictures of her with local dignitaries and her law degree. She bent over and kissed me on the cheek. "You're my backbone right now. Having you here with me is giving me the strength to do something I've been planning for weeks."

After she slid her box of stuff under the table, a white man walked in. He was dressed in a very stylish dark blue pinstriped suit. He was followed by a brother in a forest-green, double-breasted suit. The white guy looked familiar but it didn't click as to where I had seen him.

The brother's expensive suit didn't hide his skinny build and the nice haircut couldn't do a thing with that narrow head and ping-pong-ball eyes. I didn't like the look of him.

The white guy said "Daph, I hope this doesn't take long, I'm scheduled tight today." He pointed his pink stubby index finger at me and said, "Don't I know you?"

"I was thinking the same thing," I answered. Normally I extend my hand when I first meet people; shaking hands is polite. However, the minute he pointed his finger at me, politeness was no longer the protocol.

"Hmph," we both said.

The brother said nothing but kept his large eyes on me as they both joined us sitting at the card tables. Across the tables Daphne slid them each a packet of papers.

"I am leaving the firm, gentlemen. I am a partner in this firm in name only. My token days are over. I obtained a law degree to do more than attend women and minority functions.

"A couple of months ago the salary I was paid justified

my not practicing law. It made your bullshit promise to start a family law arm acceptable. It is no longer acceptable. I trust you will find the papers in order. All I'm taking from you is my name. Good day." And with that she stood and I followed.

The brother spoke first. He leaned back in one of the folding chairs, putting the chair on two legs.

"Daphne, give it a rest. You are unprepared to practice law."

"The State of Illinois says I am," she answered, clicking her black Mont Blanc ink pen closed.

"Oh please, this is drama. What, is it time for a raise or do you want a lease upgrade on your car?" the skinny bother in the suit asked.

"I want out, nothing more."

This was the battle she'd been preparing for in the car.

The white man spoke, "Daphne, you are making a grave error. Minutes ago, Martin and I were discussing a custody battle that we've decided to have you handle. It's to be your first case. You'll have the lead and Martin will assist." He smiled as if he expected those words to change her mind.

"Are you speaking of the Price case?"

"Yes," the attorney answered still smiling.

"Not interested, at least not from your table. I will be at the custody hearing however, representing Mr. Price." With a hand gesture she introduced me.

I got it. Late, but I got it. The white man was Regina's shyster and Chester's Uncle Randolph. He looked larger and taller on television. I believe he got it the same time I did, because the smile that was on his face changed—it turned kind of slimy.

"Daphne, don't do this." He stood from the chair and opened his arms as if to embrace her. "Think about your career. My God, woman, you are a new a partner in a going firm."

"Get real! You have no partners, Randolph. Martin and I are only employees. This is your show, and I want out of it." She was pointing at his chest with her ink pen, holding it more like an ice pick than a writing utensil.

"Daphne, we just put the firm name up in the reception area." He gave a hand gesture toward the front.

"Never fear, Randolph. I'm sure Kmart has more letters."

"The letters did not come from Kmart," he protested and turned to glance at them.

"Oh, excuse me. Office Max," she said.

There was a pause in the conversation. No one said a word; eyes shifted from person to person. There was nothing for me to say. I didn't have a clue as to why all the eyes settled on me.

"I have gathered my things and I'm certain you will find all the papers in order. Again, good day, gentlemen."

"Daphne, it is apparent you have sought the counsel of the ignorant in regards to this decision." His eyes were locked on me when he said, "Representing such a loser your first time out isn't advisable. Look at the facts, Daph: a security guard versus a reporter from the city's largest newspaper. Not to mention her fiancé is a respected member of Chicago's legal community. Regina will get complete custody. We will marry, and Chester will become my son."

Calm. I told myself to stay calm. He was baiting me and I knew it. Daphne placed her hand on my shoulder. I took a deep breath through my nose and let it slowly through my mouth. I stayed calm until he said, "Chester Peal . . . it has a nice ring to it don't you think?" He was talking directly to me. That was his mistake. He made it personal.

The thin brother in the green suit was between us, but I was through him in a second. Peal kept the snide smile on his face even with my hands around his neck. It wasn't until his feet left the ground that panic arrived in his eyes.

"Let him down, David! You cannot fight him from jail," Daphne said into my ear.

When I released him, he stumbled backwards to keep his footing while gasping for air. Through his gasps he muttered, "He is unstable, Daphne. He has an arrest record and is known to associate with felons. His wife has identified him as a loser, and you should too."

Backing out of the conference room, he didn't take his eyes from me. At the doorway, regaining his full voice, he said, "Convincing Daphne to help you will be of small consequence. You were an unfit husband and the court will see you as an unfit father. You should have listened to your ex-wife. See you in court, Mr. Price." He quickly backed completely out of the conference room and left.

The brother seemed uncertain if my wrath was going to be redirected toward him. He eased closer to Daphne and whispered, "Have you lost your mind, Daphne? Going against Randy on something like this isn't a smart career move. This case affects him personally. Drop it like it's hot. Forget this foolishness and come into planning with us."

"It's over, Martin." She wasn't whispering.

"Pardon?" He was asking Daphne for clarification but his eyes were on me; he was making sure he had enough room to run from the conference room if the situation called for it. He didn't have enough room.

"I'm finished with the firm and you. Our relationship is over, Martin."

He took his gaze from me to her and said, "With me? Sweetness, three weeks ago we were at the Vineyard talking engagement. Don't overreact."

"No Martin, you were talking engagement not me."

"I understand you are upset because I choose not to involve myself in your son's recent delinquent acts, and I say again, I am not the one who can help. He needs professional guidance, a behavioral specialist or something."

She looked up to me with the sweetest expression and said, "Mr. Price has agreed to help him."

Mocking, Martin asked, "Is he a licensed counselor as well as a security guard?"

The puny bastard had some balls after all. I stepped in his direction but Daphne put her hand up, stopping me. He'd taken two quick steps toward the doorway.

"No. He's only a man who wants to help my son."

"Whatever, pumpkin." His fear-filled eyes were back on me. "Let's go in with Randy and sort out this foolishness before you lose this good life."

"Oh, I'm keeping my good life. It's you and this firm that I'm getting rid of. Let's go, D."

"Daphne, no!" he raised his voice but his hands remained at his side. I wanted him to touch her. Randolph had got me in ass-kicking mode, and as of yet I was unfulfilled. Completing the task in Martin's direction was okay with me.

"I won't let you destroy your life, Daphne. I insist that you remain here with me and discuss this. Mr. Price can sit out in reception." For a second it sounded like he really did have some balls. Then Daphne started laughing at him and he reminded me of a high-school bookworm a bully had slapped upside the head. He became docile.

"We are leaving, Martin, and don't bother to call my home phone or cell. Both numbers will be changed. I will ship your things to this office."

"Is this how it ends after all I have done for you? My

Lord, Daphne, I love you. You can't leave me." The brother was copping a sincere plea.

Still laughing, Daphne pulled her box of stuff from under the card table. She snapped out the order, "Come pick this up!"

She sounded so bossy I almost moved to pick it up until I realized she was directing Martin. In a split second he was stooped beside her with the box in his grasp.

"Oh, pumpkin, you are wearing spiked heels—those are not good for your feet, you'll get a corn like before. We agreed no more spiked heels. You see, you need me, you'll hurt them without me. I won't let you take them out of my life." He was attempting to whisper but I heard him. "I love them. No, I love you, you know what I mean. I have always loved you."

He looked like he was about to start kissing her feet until she kicked at him.

"Pick the box up! Get it up and carry it to the elevator for us."

He stood with the box and said, "Please, Daphne, reconsider."

"Look, Martin I'll make a cast of them for you and mail it to you along with the photos you took of them. Okay?"

Through his face we could see his brain considering her offer.

Excitedly he asked, "You promise?"

"Ughh! Let's go, D."

# Chapter Seven

Back in my DTS, Daphne was cheesing like a six-year-old with a secret. She twisted in the car seat waiting for me to ask about the situation upstairs with the lawyers. When I pulled out of the parking garage onto LaSalle Street, I didn't ask because she was about to burst with excitement. I merely waited.

"David?"

"Yes, Attorney Nelson?"

Her being a lawyer did surprise me. Daphne was doing well for herself and I was proud of her. However, she did play me a little bit and it was only right that I play her back.

"Well?"

"Well what?" I didn't look at her because I would not have been able to keep a straight face.

"Are you okay with everything?"

"Everything?" I wanted to talk about the lawyers too, but playing with her took priority for a minute or two.

"Stop teasing me."

She shoved my shoulder, almost causing me to run up on the curb as I turned onto Congress Parkway. "Are you OK with what happened upstairs? That's a lot to have thrown at you."

Keeping a stern face and acting as if I was pondering her question, I let seconds pass before I offered, "are you asking if I'm okay with being forced to help you . . . let's see . . . dump your man, quit your job and secure, I'm guessing here, your first client?"

"Yes, David, that's what I'm asking. Are you okay with all that?"

"Humph, well that depends, are you a good lawyer?" I felt her eyes on me. Traffic came to an abrupt stop; something had the Congress blocked. We didn't merge immediately on to 94 East.

"Oh yeah I'm good, but even if I wasn't you wouldn't have anything to worry about. In a custody battle Randolph has limited if any parental rights. So . . . are you okay with everything?"

When I faced her, the insecurity in her eyes surprised me. The hardened professionalism that filled her as she had prepared to go into the lawyer's office was gone. She looked uncertain. I decided to stop playing with her because I didn't want to be responsible for the doubt I saw building in her eyes.

"Yes, I'm fine with what happened and am happy to have been there for you."

A road crew was changing the lightbulbs on the overhead street lamps. Once we passed them, traffic was clear. I mashed on the gas with authority and took the ramp leading to 94 East.

"I'm happy you were there, too. I meant what I said. It felt good to have you against my back. I haven't felt supported in long time." I heard a trembling in her voice and in the blink of an eye she was sobbing. She turned away, trying to hide the falling tears.

"What's wrong?"

She didn't answer as she cried openly. I handed her the box of Kleenex from the backseat, but her small hands were covering her eyes so she didn't take the box right away.

"David, I'm tired. Tired of it riding me down. It won't let me feel good about anything. I can be happy for moments, but it comes back on me hard, riding me down. I tried to tell myself the money was worth it. It wasn't . . . People died from me getting rich. Randolph and I, we got blood on our hands. Good people's blood."

She blew her nose hard into the Kleenex, rolled it up into a tight ball, opened her purse and dropped it in. From her purse she pulled out the slimmest gold liquor flask I had ever seen. She thumbed it open and took three small sips. She leaned the flask toward me; I declined. The aroma of cognac slipped past my nose. She flipped the top closed and said, "I'm done feeling bad for today, David. Let's talk about something else. Shall we? Where are we heading?"

The decision of whether to comment on the "it" that was riding her or proceed with conversation as if nothing was said needed to be made. Whatever the "it" was brought tears to her eyes, and seeing her crying upset me. Maybe later when I had the comforts of home to aid me, I would bring "it" up. I chose to answer her question.

"I got to swing by my office and touch base with Carol, my business partner."

"You are in business with a woman?"

"Yeah, one of the smartest people I ever met in my life."

Two trucks were riding side by side, keeping the flow of the local lanes at forty-five miles per hour. At 51st Street I switched from the local lanes to the express lanes.

"Interesting. Is she more than your business partner?"

"Yeah, she is a real friend." I knew I wasn't answering her real question. "Daphne, I've got a question for you. Why is Peal's law office so tacky looking? I thought his was a more established firm."

"Randolph is rich. The poor office look is for the clients. He gives clients the idea that he is a struggling, just-starting-out attorney. He thinks it endears him to clients. Randolph is a man only concerned with his own comforts. His private corner office is laid: wet bar, oak desk, leather chair, Tiffany lamps, Persian rugs, the whole nine yards. He plays everybody cheap—clients, staff, everybody. That's why a partnership there means nothing."

"If I hear you right, then I can assume that he is really not that big of a threat."

"Oh no, David, Attorney Randolph Peal is a rich man with pull. Don't get it twisted. He is a very real threat."

"And you can fight him?"

"We can fight him, as long as we work together, support each other and have each other's back." She rested her head against my shoulder.

Quiet minutes passed. I wondered if the "it" was back on her mind. Without realizing it, I had the DTS up to ninety-five miles per hour. I eased off the gas, slowing the sedan down. We were at 83rd Street. I exited and headed to the office. I rolled the windows halfway down and let the late morning air blow through the car.

"I have been watching my own back for a long time, David. Ever since I've been grown, I've been supporting myself. No man has ever really supported me, really had my back. I used men, but I couldn't depend on them." She sat straight up and looked at me. "Understand?"

"No, you are going to have to explain that one, baby. You used men but didn't depend on them?"

"Okay, for example, Martin advised me to invest in an emerging dot-com company. I did it and made money. Does that mean Martin had my back? No. I used the advice he gave me to make money; that's not support. The money I made from his suggestion does not pay my light bill. I paid my light bill before I invested the money. You follow?"

"No."

"I depend on my lights, they are not a luxury. Lights, food and utilities are necessities. No one pays them but me. I don't trust another person to pay them because I need them. What I need, I must take care of myself. Follow me?"

I didn't have a clue. Therefore I didn't answer. She continued.

"This is support: if I wrenched my back and leaned on you, you would help me walk. If I wrenched my back around Martin, I would have to crawl my ass to the doctor.

"A month ago I told Martin I wasn't happy with my position at the firm. I asked him if he would go in with me and talk to Randolph about bringing in family law cases. He told me that would be rocking the boat and refused. With him as my man, I stood alone. Getting it? No?

"Okay, try this. I needed Martin to help me with my son, I needed his support. He refused. He flat-out said it was out of his area of expertise. When Stanley was a little boy he didn't have a bike, it wasn't like we couldn't buy him a bike, because we—Mama, me or Daddy—could have got him one, but for some reason he didn't have one. You gave him an old one from your garage and taught him how to ride it. I didn't ask you to do that, you just stepped up and did it."

When I swung around a three-legged dog was on 83rd Street that obviously wasn't afraid of getting hit by a car;

Daphne let out a little chirp for the dog, but continued with her thought.

"Martin got Randolph to pay for my schooling, but never went to the library with me, never watched Stanley for me when I had to study and never offered to help with one research paper. I used Martin, but I didn't depend on him. Understand?"

"Yes, I believe I do. I need you to help me keep my son. I'm leaning on you and by helping me you are offering support. Is that right?"

"Yeah, you got it. We are supporting each other. Most people can't always follow my line of thought and I do have a problem with thinking ahead. The minute I heard you say you were looking for a lawyer, I started laying out the courtroom argument before you even agreed to my taking the case."

"Do I hear you saying you have a plan?"

"Oh yes, I most certainly do." She turned in her seat to completely face me. "Would you like to hear it?"

"Of course I would." At the stoplight on Vincennes, I looked to my right and noticed that they had almost finished renovating the old warehouse that would be the new Simeon Vocational High School.

"I believe all of Randolph's talk of adoption is to impress Regina. She is the prize in Randolph's eyes, not Chester. My plan is to get Regina into family court before they're married. Once she sees how seriously the court looks upon keeping knowledge of a child's birth away from the biological father, she'll conform to your wishes."

"You sound confident."

"David you know as well as I, Regina is not a fool. Randolph has got her confused. The reality of the law will bring clarity to her mind. Please believe."

I really would like to know how he got her confused.

The years I was married to her, she was one of the most focused, goal-oriented people I'd met in my life.

A white Bentley made the turn with us at 83rd street, the car was on Daphne's side, so I didn't get a clear look at the driver. All I heard was the yelled threat, "Bitch you is as good as dead!"

Then the Bentley's driver pulled ahead of us, cut me off and slammed on his brakes, causing me to slam on mine. He then sped away fast enough to make the next light and a right at the far corner, leaving me dumfounded and confused.

"Are you all right?" I asked, pulling myself back from the dashboard.

"I'm fine." She exhaled and closed her eyes.

I pulled up to the light. "Who was that, baby? Did you know him?"

"No, but the car looked familiar," she said worriedly.

"Associates of Stanley, maybe?"

"Not in a Bentley."

Who was really in danger was my thought. Was I being hired to protect her or her son? Obviously more was going on than I had been told, which is often the case in the protection business. You never find out the severity of the threat until you're in with both feet.

# Chapter Eight

My office of five years was located on the corner of 87th and Throop Street. When I first moved in, only a dentist occupied the whole building. The second floor was all storage. Three months ago, following Carol's advice, we bought the building. Within two months, she'd cleaned out, spruced up and rented the whole second floor.

We are now landlords to three rent-paying businesses, which covered the mortgage and left us with a hefty monthly profit. Carol sees her way to profit quickly. The woman counts money in her sleep, which is why I made her my partner.

When Daphne and I entered the office, we were greeted by the pleasant odor of tropical-blend potpourri. Carol had hidden a crock-pot half filled with simmering potpourri flakes, and it kept the office smelling fresh.

Carol walked up from the back of the office and met us with a smile and a nod. She was on the phone. In her right ear was the tiny headset she used to answer the phone.

She was dressed in her standard high-collared white lace blouse and a two-piece skirt suit. The rich purple color of the suit complemented her Hershey-brown skin.

Our office is divided in half. One half, I would say, is professionally chic. The other side, my area, needed a little work. Carol had her side flowing to a feng shui–type groove. She has a flat black tabletop desk, with no drawers and a slender black high-back leather chair that glided rather than rolled.

The office, phone, fax and e-mail all are routed though her computer. Her computer screen is thinner than my .9mm pistol. Everything on her side is aligned, from the plant in her corner to the rug under her thin desk. My side is a little different.

I started this business with a prayer, an unemployment check and a promise to pay my first month's rent. The first shopping I did was at the flea market. A guy there sold me an old-fashioned schoolteacher's desk made of pine, along with a tin wastebasket, a florescent desk lamp and a spring-cushioned high-back wicker office chair that rocked back and locked. My side ain't pretty, but it's comfortable.

After I paid to have the office phone lines installed and the lights cut on, it was ramen noodles and saltines for weeks. The desk served as a reminder of when things weren't prosperous and the sacrifice it took to get here. I have a tendency to forget how blessed I am and become ungrateful. My less-than-chic side of the office helps me keep it real.

After Carol disconnected from her call, I said, "Hey there, Ms. Carol Anne Cooper."

"Hey there yourself, Mr. David Price." Her thin, slanted eyes were smiling. Cat eyes, Ricky calls them. However, at that moment they reminded one more of kitten eyes, a happy kitten at that. Something had Carol delighted.

"Carol, this is Attorney Daphne Nelson. She has agreed to help with a situation that has developed."

She extended her hand and a big smile to Daphne. "It's good to see you again! We met at the fall fashion show last weekend at the DuSable museum. Remember?"

"Oh, girl, yes; that was you!" Now both women were smiling like happy kittens. They hugged, giggled and damn near broke out in a cheer. "Oh, I haven't laughed at people like that since high school."

My office is made up of two rooms and a hallway. The front area is the largest room, eighteen by sixteen feet. It's almost a perfect square. The women were standing in the middle of the square.

"The lady in the yellow, I swear I saw her two days later at the restaurant Nine, in that same chicken outfit."

"Hush!"

"Mm, wearing it like Vera Wang christened it herself. She was just as Prada proud as she wanted to be in that knockoff."

I had never heard Carol signifying on someone and wasn't aware that she frequented fashion shows. The women were leaning on each other shoulder to shoulder. They were close to the same height and complexion, with Carol being slightly shorter and darker. Ricky calls her a "Chocolate China Doll," which usually gets him hissed at.

"Yesterday I received an invitation to a showing at Nordstrom. Interested?"

"Girl, I was confirming two seats as you and David were walking in. I was going to call my tired cousin and invite her, but I would much rather go with you. Meet you there three-thirty Sunday?"

"It's a date."

"Don't be late."

More giggles.

Carol was my first case after I got my license, and the first person to call in response to the ten thousand flyers Ricky and I distributed by hand. The flyers were Ricky's idea. Being that he had started up three successful businesses on his own, I valued Ricky's opinion. Besides, he paid to have them printed. Seventy percent of my first year's business came through those flyers.

Carol's call was in response to the flyers I'd passed out at the Jewel grocery store on 94th and Ashland. When she called, she asked me was I serious and could I really protect her from someone trying to hurt her. Motivated by being broke, I told her I could protect her from Satan himself. She believed me.

Satan for her was Nicholas Baines, her abusive, unemployed and ignorant husband of three years. Carol wanted him out of her apartment and out of her life. Nicholas had beaten Carol into believing that if she called the police he would kill her.

When we actually met, Carol was under the misguided impression that my services were that of a hired killer. She wanted a contract on dude and didn't try to hide her disappointment when I explained what a security escort did.

Carol is maybe 105 pounds on her heavy days. Nicholas outweighed her by his ponytail; he couldn't have weighed more than 110 pounds. I went to her apartment, packed up his belongings and threw them and him out on the streets. I stayed with her for three days.

He came back once. I took off my belt and beat him, then slung him down two flights of stairs. He twisted his leg pretty bad on the bottom flight. I was going to help him up until Carol pushed past me with a cast-iron skillet in her hand. She went upside that man's head with a vengeance.

She broke his nose and his jaw. I had to restrain her so he could crawl out of the vestibule. I thought she had calmed herself, so I let her go. She broke out the front door, jumped in her day-care job's minivan and tried to run him down. If I had not jumped in front of him, she would have run him over.

After I stopped her from running him over I was convinced he was gone for good, so a brother went home. The next day I was watching the news and saw Carol and Nicholas on the screen. She'd run him down with the day care's minivan and backed over him twice, killing him. The police found the .380 pistol in his hand that he used to shoot three bullet holes through her windshield.

The police kept Carol for a week because of mixed reports from eyewitnesses. Some said he was running from her and firing back at the van. Others said he stood in front of the van and fired on her when she got in it. The majority of the witnesses said Nicholas was running for his life.

After getting to know Carol, I personally believe she saw him walking down her block, possibly heading to her place, and she ran him down. Once she saw he wasn't Satan on Earth, she wanted some of that ass.

In the end she was cleared of all charges. To pay for my services, she wrote me a check—which bounced because the day care she was working for fired her due to the incident and ensuing bad press. She brought me a proposition that said, "Since I owe you and since you really do need some help, why don't I work here?"

Truthfully, it was guilt that initially made me say yes. I felt like it was my fault Nicholas returned, but hiring her turned out to be the best business decision I have ever made.

The two chatty women walked over and stood in front of Carol's desk. Daphne asked, "Is that your gold Benz parked on the side street?"

"Yes. You like?"

"Girl, I drive one just like it!"

"No!"

"I do. I do!"

"Girl, we are too much alike."

"Stylish minds think on time!"

"Similar taste, don't wait."

Then they both cut their eyes to me.

"Tall and thick," Carol said, whispering with a little laugh.

What was wrong with Carol? She'd never made such a comment before, at least not to my knowledge. Why all of a sudden was she looking at me like she wanted to put a dollar in my briefs? We had a good working relationship with no hanky-panky or hints of hanky-panky.

"Long and thick is more like it," Daphne said, barely audible.

"Pardon!" Carol was no longer giggling, nor was she whispering.

All laughter stopped, and the giggling, cheerful mood of the room changed. The women locked eyes and then they rolled them at each other. Each looked at me as if I was supposed to say something.

Just a few moments before they were all private with their stuff, now they wanted to involve me, but it wasn't happening. I acted like I didn't hear or see anything and left. I walked to the back of the office under the pretense of fixing espresso.

The back room is the smaller of the two rooms of my office. Ten by twelve, it's sort of the kitchen/storeroom. We've got a sink, a microwave, a counter and an espresso machine. Walking to the back I heard Carol ask, "So where did you meet David?"

"I've known him for years. He was my neighbor in Harvey, and he was married to one of my best friends, Regina."

"I see. Well what brings you to our office today?"

"David and I are working on something."

"Really? Is it related to Epsilon Security Service?"

"He's helping me with my son."

"Is he protecting your son?"

"Yes."

"Great! I love new business. Please have a seat and I'll pull together the necessary papers."

There was only one word to describe my actions: cowardly. I stayed in the back while they ironed out whatever was going on between them. I turned on the espresso machine so they would think I couldn't hear them talking, and it was noisy enough to stop either of them from calling me.

I had all intentions of telling Carol this case was to be a trade-out, involving only my time and limiting the use of Epsilon man-hours. I was expecting her to balk a little, but once I explained how my son was involved, I figured she'd go along. The change in her tone of voice told me a trade would be a problem. She wanted money from Daphne.

Last night, Daphne did agree to pay for my service. However, that was before her confession of "togetherness." I could pull senior partner rank and demand a trade, but the price of that type of move wouldn't be paid for months. I have learned to pick my battles with Carol.

Standing there listening to the espresso machine gurgle, it occurred to me that Daphne would be collecting a fee as well, since I was her first client. After all, she needed billing hours. She'd pay me and I would pay her. With a workable solution in mind, I returned to the front.

"What, no espresso?" That was Carol, commenting on the fact that I came back empty-handed. She sat behind her desk, smiling, not the happy kitten smile of before, but a satisfied cat-that-ate-the-mouse smile. Atop the agreement papers on her desk was a pastel-colored check.

"Ms. Nelson has secured protection for one Stanley Nelson for seven days. She has informed me that you extended services last night and this morning. The contract starts today; last night's service will not be billed."

The amount of the check indicated that Carol charged the higher of our two rates. We have the standard rate that's printed on all our marketing material and we have what I like to call our 'hood' rate which is not printed anywhere. It's the rate for folks in a lot of need with only a little cash.

"Did Daphne inform you that she is the attorney representing me in a matter that developed last night?" I slid behind my monstrosity of a desk and looked across to the two very good-looking women. The dark brown skin colors with the purple and silver was striking. They kind of looked like models sitting over there, slim, petite models.

"No, we only spoke of Epsilon Security Service business. What occurred last night that caused you to need a lawyer?" Carol clicked the cap back on her own Mont Blanc ink pen, which I bought her for Christmas.

"Regina is planning to marry and wants her prospective husband to adopt Chester."

"No! Why would she want that?" Carol asked honestly shocked.

"I'm not certain."

"She's under Randolph's influence," Daphne offered while sliding her checkbook inside her purse. Daphne crossed her legs and bobbed her foot.

"Randolph?"

"He's the white attorney she's thinking of marrying."

"Do you mean white as in Caucasian?"

"Yes," I answered.

"Oh, I see. So how are you going to help David?" she asked Daphne.

With her foot still bobbing, Daphne answered, "The plan is to take Regina to court before the marriage and establish guardianship."

Carol looked at me with her eyes thinning, and in an accusing tone asked, "What did you do to her, David? I don't see Regina doing a thing like this."

"I did nothing to her!"

With ink pen pointing, she surmised, "You had to do something, David. She chose to involve you in Chester's life when you didn't even know he existed. Why would the same woman try to remove you from his life?"

I started not to answer her evil-sounding self. She was supposed to be on my side. "She's not trying to remove me from his life. I can visit Chester whenever I want. She wants him to have Randolph's last name, making him an heir to his wealth."

"Oh," she paused, "now that sounds like Regina. She has always been about the dollars. I can see her suggesting something along those lines."

The two women nodded in agreement. They were about to give each other five, but stopped short.

"What are y'all agreeing about? What she's trying to do is wrong!"

"We are not lessening the wrong in her actions, David, but it does sound like a Gina move," Carol said.

"A Gina move?"

"She's right, David. It is a Gina move. Over the last couple of years, Regina has been making some serious power moves. Especially financially. Sister girl been going off!

The stock market, the sale of her property, her pension rollover and even her venture capital investments have been paying off big; everything she touches has been yielding her tens of thousands of dollars. Gina has been making some moves!" Daphne extended her palm and this time they gave each other dap.

"So her offering my son to a white man is a power move?"

"For the boy it is. For him it's a win-win situation. He gets you raising him and inherits a rich man's wealth; from Regina's perspective not a bad thing for her son."

I couldn't tell if Daphne was teasing or if she really agreed with Gina.

"He is my son, okay? My son should have my name!"

"That sounds like a lot of male ego to me. I mean think about it, your name isn't really yours. It's a hand-me-down from slavery. How much pride is there really in carrying a slave master's name for some two hundred and forty or so years? Is your last name really that important to you?"

I started to get ugly and comment on her son not having his father's name, but I didn't. "My daddy gave me my name."

"He could have given you diabetes. Would you be proud of that too?"

"You're tripping, Daphne."

In her own defense she offered, "No, I am just trying to get you to see it from a different perspective. A battle is fought better if you can gain your adversary's view."

"So you saying it's all about money with Gina?"

"As far as I can see; she's not denying you visitation. She wants you to be part of Chester's life."

"You honestly think that Regina sees no wrong in what she is doing?"

"It's not about an emotional right and wrong for Gina.

It's about a financial right and wrong, and it would be financially wrong for her not to let Randolph adopt Chester."

With that statement, I saw how important wealth really was to Daphne.

"I'm not a poor man."

"You're not a poor man by a working-class man's standards, but you're broke by Randolph's standards. He has an estate in Olympia Fields and is building another in Lake Forest. His downtown condominium is a tri-level on Oak Street. A financial Goliath is trying to adopt your son." Daphne flipped opened her two-way and checked an incoming message.

The room was quiet. I guess she was allowing her point to sink in.

The front office door was pushed open. A County sheriff walked in asking for David Price. Carol pointed to me. He handed me a folded piece of paper. When I opened it, I saw it was a restraining order, barring me from being within 150 feet of Attorney Randolph Peal. I showed it to Daphne.

"It's started. He's got you on record as a threat. He's attacking your character on paper."

"What do we do?"

"We get Regina in court." When Daphne flipped her two-way pager closed her cell phone rang. The ringer sounded to the Marvin Gaye song, "Let's Get it On."

She indicated by mouthing that it was Martin on the line. He wanted to meet with her. She told him he could meet with us. He hesitated, but agreed when he understood she wasn't going to give. I suggested she bring him out south to us. I didn't feel like driving back downtown. We agreed to Jackie's, a soul food restaurant on 71st and Vernon three hours later.

Off the phone, Daphne told us she delayed meeting with him because she wanted to secure a court date as soon as possible, and whatever Martin wanted to discuss could wait until that was done.

The office phone rang. Carol answered. It was for me, and she put the call on speaker. It was my cleaning service; apparently the young man in my home was directing them to wash windows and clean silverware. I laughed and I told them no, their normal duties would suffice. Stanley was trying to delegate his responsibilities. I liked that in the kid.

# Chapter Nine

We drove from the office to my house with very little conversation. I parked behind Daphne's gold Benz and watched the sun's rays dance with the metallic flake chips in the car's paint. The Benz was sparkling.

I hadn't paid much attention to Carol's. I was simply happy that she'd gotten something nice for herself. But looking at Daphne's, I realized that it wasn't only a nice car; it was a fly ride. Carol was getting kind of jazzy.

I rested my head against the headrest and looked up through my sunroof. The afternoon sky was clear and blue. Thank God the humidity had dropped and given us a break from the heavy sweating, but it remained hot. I was anxious to get out of my suit, because light wool is wool all the same.

"Did you know you and Martin drive the same kind of car?"

"He drives a Caddy?"

"Yeah, the same model as this one, identical color and everything. Don't you find it interesting that both our partners match? Look at it, I was a partner with Martin at the firm and he drives a black DTS. You are a partner with Carol and she drives a gold C class. You have to admit there may be something cosmic to it. Perhaps we should hook the two of them up?"

"No, I want no parts of Martin in my life."

"Well don't rule it out. Carol is going to need someone once she finds out you're going to need her less in your life."

"Carol and I aren't . . ."

"David, please, a woman senses what a man doesn't. You may not be cognizant of it, but Carol has got plans for you. Please believe." She reached over and held my hand. "I need to explain something to you. Well not explain, but tell you something. It's related to my outburst last night and earlier today."

I imagined it was the "it" that was riding her down. "Wouldn't you rather talk inside the house?"

"Yes, of course. I would like to get something out of my car before we go in."

Hers was the only Benz on the block. Looking up and down, I had to admit our block looked good for being in the hood. There were small neat lawns, chain link fences, hedges and no abandoned or raggedy houses on the block. A group of kids were rolling out a basketball hoop and that would be the center of all they did that day. Despite the heat, they played ball all day long.

They set the hoop in front of the only dope house. There was a time we had three, but with concerned neighbors and a cop moving onto the block, two left. The Reeds, the owners of the one that remained, had lived on the block as long as my family.

As a child I remember my grandmother's referring to the house as the policy house. When I was teenager, that was where I brought my first dime bag of weed, and as a man, that was where I dragged my crack-addicted brother Robert from more times than I cared to remember.

The Reeds and I are the only homeowners who don't complain about the kids setting up the basketball hoop in front of our houses. I don't complain because I like to watch them hoop. The Reeds, the kids tell me, don't complain about anything, as long as it doesn't stop the traffic from coming and going out their back door.

Daphne went to the trunk of her car and pulled out a large legal hanging file filled with newspapers. I reached to help her, but she backed away. "I got it, David."

When we walked into the house I halfway expected to smell a blunt burning, hear Nelly blasting in the background and see a group of teens chilling on my couch. Much to my comfort, none of that happened. Stanley was stretched out on the couch, asleep. He did, however, have the big screen on the Playboy channel. Yin and Yang sat watching intently; they looked over their shoulder to us, then back to the screen.

The mahogany box that held my grandmother's silverware was on the coffee table, open, along with the silver polish and rags. The pieces gleamed from the box. Daphne signaled for us to leave Stanley sleeping. We eased by him into the kitchen.

She placed the papers at her feet as she sat at the table. "On second thought, I am not entirely ready to share this information with you."

"No problem, baby." And it really wasn't. My mind was spinning with my own problems. I wanted the relief of a cold shower and the freedom of my Nike shorts.

"But I am positive it will be helpful with us in dealing with Randolph if things go that far. After we speak with Martin, I'll know better how to handle it. If you don't mind, I would like to use your phone to try and get us a court date this week."

"Please feel free."

Trying not to wake up Stanley, I quietly called the dogs to the back door and let them out in the yard. Standing on the back porch at the screen I watched them wrestle in the grass while different thoughts crossed my mind.

How important was my last name?

Was it a male ego thing?

Was I denying Chester a chance at a better life?

If it was a rich black man wanting to adopt him would I protest as much?

Price is a family name and a tag from slavery. For most African-Americans a family name is both, but it's a family name all the same. My family name, thereby my family history. I could go back only to my granddaddy, who didn't know his daddy and didn't care that he didn't know him. All he ever told me about his mama was that she taught him to count money. There is not a whole lot of history attached to my family name, but what's there belongs to us. The Prices.

As a boy I was proud to be a Price. It used to make me feel good to hear one of Daddy's buddies say, "There go one of them Price boys, tell ya daddy I said hey." It was pretty much the same at church. I wasn't David and my brothers weren't Robert or Charles. We were all, "them Price boys" or "one of those Price boys." At the barbershop they called my granddaddy, my father, me and my brothers Price. We were all Price.

As a child I understood that people knew my family and I felt good about that. My father wasn't my mama's "baby's daddy," he was my father, and I had his name.

My daddy and my granddaddy set standards for us to follow: "A Price does this, a Price does that." I was raised as a Price. My father was part of me and I he. There was comfort in knowing that I was a Price, and my son should have that same security.

Financially, I could provide for my son better than I was provided for. True, I might not be wealthy by Peal's standard, but I could take care of mine. If it was male ego, so be it. It was only right that I should give my son what was given to me. My son would have the strength and confidence of a family name.

It was the Marvin Gaye ringtone of Daphne's phone, which pulled me from my thoughts.

"It's Randolph's cell number on my screen. Should I answer?" she asked loudly from the kitchen.

"Yeah, see what he wants." I walked from the back door into the kitchen and sat in the chair next to her.

"Yes, Randolph, how can I help you?" Her tone was guarded, almost fearful. Her leg nervously tapped against the file of newspapers at her feet.

"Yes, I understand we have a history together . . . I disagree. I don't see my leaving as disloyal. I am doing what is best for me . . . What? . . . Randolph I would never, that would hurt us both . . . you shouldn't view my moving on as a threat to you . . . David had nothing to do with my decision . . . that's not your business . . . if you consider me a threat, there is nothing I can do about it . . . no, I don't consider you a threat . . . what? Yes, I am sure we will both meet there and the only bitch I know is your mother!" She flipped the phone closed.

"I should have known it wasn't going to happen that easy. He's afraid. As long as I was with him, under his watch, he was cool. Sinners are bound by secrets, and now that I am away from him, he is afraid I will break our bond."

"Are you afraid of him?"

"Not the way he fears me. He's afraid I will ruin him, and I fear what he will do to stop that from happening."

"I won't let him hurt you."

"D, I'm not going to give him a reason to hurt me. I got the court date set for Friday morning. If all goes well, Regina will come to her senses and this will all be over."

At that moment Stanley entered the kitchen, "Hey, Ma what's going on? I just got a two-way from Martin, saying he's going to give you my last check and that we are finished doing business. What's up with that?"

"I'm going into practice on my own."

"Are you going to do crash cases?"

"No!" Her jaws set and her teeth clenched.

"Then why is Martin ending my thang?"

"Baby," she massaged her own temples bringing some release to her tight face, "I'm ending your thang, okay? I'm taking you out of the crash case business."

"Ma, I ain't got enough to get my ride."

"No, but together I'm sure we have enough to get you a nice little car, that will get you back and forth from school."

"Ma! I was getting a whip, not a nice little car."

"We are through talking now, Stan. Leave Mr. Price and me alone for a second."

"Ma!"

"Go on up front boy! We'll talk later."

He slumped out the kitchen.

Trying my hand at a little levity I say, "The boy said he wants a whip, girl. Not a nice car."

"Yeah, well, his and my wants are going to be on hold awhile. But talking to him made me think about a person who might be the answer to our problems—that is if things go south with Randolph."

"Who?"

"The person he hurt most with our shared sin; his ex-wife Eleanor."

I wanted to ask her what the sin was, but life had taught me that patience is indeed a virtue. "I know his first wife, Eleanor Jackson. Her family is from Englewood. Nice folks. I went to her parents' wedding; they had lived together over twenty years and then got married. Man that was a big event; they hired two bands and a DJ, reserved half the park and had enough food to feed the whole south side of town. Eleanor and I talked a great deal at the wedding. I like her. Does she know the secret?"

"No, if she did, Randolph would be ruined. She wouldn't hesitate to nail his behind to the wall. Please believe. I need to call her anyway and tell her I made the move away from Randolph. She'll be happy."

"You and her are friends?"

"Yeah, she's my girl. I met her when I was going to Roosevelt University. She was a serious student, always telling me I couldn't afford to play like the white kids. She would say, "We are young black females, a rarity at this level; playtime is over." She preached harder than my parents, but I didn't hear her. We got cool regardless of my poor study habits and partying. She went straight through and got a paralegal certificate; me, I dropped out of the paralegal program, but I went back a couple of years later for my bachelor's.

"After she graduated, she started a data-entry service, and once I started with Randolph, I got him to send her some business. They eventually started dating, and one thing led to another, and they got married."

Daphne cut off her two-way pager and put it in her purse. She stood, yawned and stretched toward the ceiling, slid out of her suit coat and hung it on the back of the chair, then sat back at the table with me.

She wore a camisole with no bra. I didn't want to be distracted. A brother had to muster up enough self-restraint to ask a hard question.

"If she's your girl, why haven't you shared the information with her?"

She looked down at her manicured nails. Her eyes came back to me, then to the wall behind me and finally back to me.

"Because I'm as guilty as Randolph, that's why. The information would cause her to hate me too."

Marvin Gaye sounded off again and Daphne flipped her phone open. It was Martin confirming our meeting. We had over an hour before we were to meet him at Jackie's.

After she'd confirmed and hung up, I asked, "So what's the deal with you and Martin?"

"Attorney Martin MacNard, my man, excuse me, my ex-man. Didn't you think he was all that and a bag of chips?"

"No."

She patted my knee. "Well, he thinks he is. The man loves himself."

"Sounds like he loves you."

"Please, he's a foot freak. He has a foot fetish. He loves my feet." She reached down and slipped her high heels off. "The man will do anything I tell him as long as I allow him to rub, kiss and pamper my feet. In the beginning it was kind of erotic, until I found out his toe sucking wasn't foreplay. He achieves a climax from sucking my toes."

"No!"

"It's the truth. Over the years we've been together I can count the times we had actual sexual intercourse. He's not one for copulation. He'd rub on himself and suck my toes till satisfied." She placed her feet in my lap. They were pretty.

"Was he unable to get erect?"

"No not at all, he got good and hard at the drop of a hat, or should I say, the drop of a shoe. Whenever I slid my shoes off a lump would start going in his trousers. Do you mind rubbing my feet a little, these aren't my walking shoes?"

I'm good at foot massages, but I use them for foreplay and since the bedroom wasn't on the schedule that afternoon, all I did was rub her feet.

"How long were you with him?"

"Well, I met him while bird-dogging for Randolph. He was an impressive young African-American attorney with ambition. To me he was all that and a bag of chips. He convinced Randolph to pay for my last year at Roosevelt and all of my law school. What's that, five years? He's been leaving me with wet toes for five years."

"Why did you stay with him?"

"He did for me, and Randolph thought it was a good idea. There was a time when Randolph's words were gold to me. Whatever he suggested, this girl did. It was Randolph who put me onto the first real money that came my way.

"I was driving Daddy's raggedy Ford Tempo when a beer truck ran me into a storefront. I wasn't injured, but the fire department did have to cut me out of the car. An ambulance took me to the hospital. While they were rolling me in, Randolph popped up on the side of the gurney and asked me if I had a lawyer. I said no. He told me I was wrong and that he was my lawyer.

"The next thing I knew, I was in another ambulance going to a hospital out in the western suburbs. Three weeks later when I got out of the hospital, Randolph paid me fifteen thousand dollars. When the beer company settled, I got a new Volvo and another ten thousand.

"I gave my daddy two grand and moved out. I started

bird-dogging, that's recruiting people to be in staged accidents, in case you didn't know what bird-dogging was, for Randolph full time.

"He had full-time dispatchers who monitored police, fire, and ambulance calls for legitimate accident-victim clients. Randolph put a two-way radio in my car and bought me some business suits. Then he taught me what to say to people who had just been pulled from a wreck and were on their way to a hospital. He taught me how to console and offer wealth all in one sentence. Randolph plugged me in. I was taking care of my son, my folks and me.

"Every eighteen months or so I would be in an accident and get a big check. I started buying property with the big checks. The first house I bought was my daddy's. He had two mortgages on a house he got with a VA loan. He wept tears of joy when I put the deed on his dresser.

"When Martin came into my life, I thought I was financially secure, my property was taking care of me; he showed me different. He taught me money management. And he showed me how educated wealthy people lived. I became as wealthy as an educated professional, but I wasn't educated and in the company of the educated, so I felt inferior.

"When Martin and I started dating, he took me to events I ignored in the past: galas, political functions, charitable events and society weddings. Our pictures were popping up in newspapers and local magazines. I was traveling in the same circles as Regina and her mother. That's how Regina's and my friendship got started. We continued to run into each other.

"After one of the mayor's parties I mentioned to Martin that I felt undereducated among his crowd. He agreed that I was and to show that he lived in the 'solution and not the problem,' he promised to get all my tuition paid, undergraduate and graduate if I so desired.

"My mother didn't raise a fool, D. I went back to school and got my law degree. Was it worth five years of wet toes? Yes, in the long run it was."

"Why did you dump him?"

"Baby, please, why didn't I dump him sooner is the question. The graduate education changed my outlook on life. I try not to settle, D. It leaves one unsatisfied. This morning you gave me satisfaction in areas of my life that have been pruned by settling. My law degree caused me to think larger, to grow. I've grown past settling.

"I refuse to be with a man who doesn't care about my son. I am not settling for a man who doesn't respect me, nor am I settling for a man who would rather lick my toes than my clit. Life is too good for settling. Five years of wet toes is enough. I am now a practicing attorney and more than capable of finding a man who knows how to satisfy me." She winked at me.

"Oh yeah, sounds like you saying I knocked the brother out of the box?"

"Maybe." Her feet dropped from my lap. She pressed her full lips against my neck, sucked on my flesh, then repeated, "Maybe."

I checked my Rolex to see if there was enough time to go under her camisole; there wasn't. The meeting with Martin was less than twenty minutes away.

Jackie's had been one of my favorite places to meet and eat for years. They cook like my family. The crispy salmon croquettes we ordered, along with the pan-fried cornbread, okra and peas, and even the hand-squeezed lemonade; all would have easily been at home on my mother's table.

The folks who patronize Jackie's restaurant come to eat; there is not a lot eavesdropping when the food is good. I'd allowed Stanley to drive us over to the restaurant. He enjoyed chauffeuring us, and was in a pretty good mood behind it. He'd said he'd driven a Caddy just like mine before. Martin's I guessed.

Sitting in a booth waiting for our food, Stanley turned to his mother and said, "Ma, I'm sorry for lying to you about the money. I was scared. I only tried to take your money because I knew I had money coming from Martin. If you would have given it to me, I would have paid you back. Fo' real, Ma. And as soon as Martin gives me the check, I'm going to call dude and this is all going to be over with." He directed his words to me and asked, "Mr. Price, would you go with me to pay dude?"

"That's what your mother hired me for, son." I thought about the check Daphne wrote for a week's worth of protection and smiled. Carol owed her a refund.

Daphne, Stanley and I were discussing who was going to walk over and pick a selection from the jukebox, when Martin entered. He slid into the booth next to Stanley.

Daphne told him we'd ordered. He looked around at the soul food restaurant's decor, snubbed it and decided not to order. Once our food came, however, he changed his mind, and had the waitress bring him a menu.

Martin didn't strike me as a short ribs, greens and macaroni and cheese type of brother, but that's what he ordered. Nor did he strike me as a brother who licked his fingers, but he did, and that brought laughter from the three of us.

"Pardon me for that, it's been a while since I have had food . . . like . . . well prepared in such a fashion."

"Had a flashback, huh? Went back to the days when you used to chew on chicken gristle and sop biscuits, huh? Don't worry. We won't tell anybody." I winked at him.

He took his paper napkin from his lap and tossed it onto

his plate as if he were angry, but the brother had eaten too good to be mad, and I knew it.

"Yes, well as pleasant as it may have been, shall we deal with the matter at hand? Your desertion from the firm," he said to Daphne.

"What desertion? Martin, please, I resigned. I quit. It was a job. People leave employers all the time."

"Not ones who have been as good to you as Randolph. Woman, he brought you from the depths of the hood. Through us you became educated and wealthy."

"*Us?* Are you joined at the hip with him?"

"Not the hip, dear . . . the wallet—the same as you."

"Martin, things happened before you came to the firm, things that you don't know about."

"No darling, there are things you think I don't know about . . ." Both were trying to probe the other for information through the eyes. Nothing passed between them. Martin reached into his suit coat. "Here is Stanley's check. Note, I included commissions from his last case, as well as the one he has pending."

"Cool!" was Stanley's reply reaching for the check.

"Getting rid of us, Martin?" Daphne asked.

"No, it's you leaving, and since your decision is made, I see no need in having loose threads. Clean and neat is best."

Daphne took the check from Stanley's grasp, "Randolph didn't send a message?"

"Not by me, dear. This meeting is between us. I saw no need to mention it to Randolph."

"The only reason you wanted to meet was to bring us Stanley's check?"

"And to add closure. Seeing you here . . . at this . . . dining establishment with him, permits me to observe you in an environment that better suits you. The lifestyle I offered was too much pressure for someone of your . . . social background. I realize that now. A simpler, slower pace is what you required, and I wish you all the best."

Daphne snickered. She bent her head to his ear and very quietly said, "You pretentious toe-sucking freak, you best to leave before I show you how simplistic and slow I really am and rise up from here and slap you upside your motherfucking head."

The southside came out of the girl, and ran him up out the joint. Martin left without a word and without paying for his meal.

With Martin gone, Daphne's and my attention turned to Stanley. She laid the check on the table and handed him her cell phone. He didn't hesitate to make the call.

"Yeah what's up family, it's me, Snap . . . Yeah, I got your loot . . . I can get it to you tonight . . . Me and my uncle will meet you at the McDonald's on 47th and Cottage Grove . . . Naw, he ain't the police . . . Awight, see you at eight, peace."

After Stanley disconnected, I asked; "Why didn't you meet him now?"

"His mama at work and ain't nobody there to watch his little brothers and sisters."

I wanted to, but Daphne did it. She broke out in laughter. The threatening gangster had to baby-sit. She took her cell phone from Stanley and called Eleanor.

"Girl where are you? . . . Bernice just finished your hair, so you're close by us . . . we're at Jackie's . . . girl it's only 3:50 . . . you can run over here . . . why should we drive all the way out there if you right here by us? . . . child that is too extra for me . . . Okay, I see your point, but have Michael open the back gate. I'm not with going through your forest to get to you. Love you too, babe." She flipped the phone closed and looked to Stanley and me. "Yes, it's a bit out of our plans for today, but I need to talk with her. I hope you gentlemen don't mind?"

"No," we gentlemen answered.

"Good, because I need to stop by the house first. I bought Eleanor something from Martha's Vineyard, and this is the perfect time to give it to her."

# Chapter Ten

It wasn't like I forgot about protecting Stanley; however it wasn't at the forefront of my mind. We were about to walk up the back steps of Daphne and Stanley's home when I saw the back door was wide open.

"Did you leave your door open?" I asked Daphne

"No."

Straightaway I pulled Stanley and Daphne behind me and yanked free one of the two .9mm guns that were strapped to my person. Before I could take the first step up, Randolph appeared at the door above. He saw us and stopped cold.

In his hands he was carrying a small fire safe. Under his arms were files, and dangling from his mouth was what looked like a house key.

"Hey, Daph," he said through clenched teeth.

Daphne pushed past me, walked up the steps and snatched the key from his mouth.

"This is Martin's key! That's why he met with us? To give you time to break into my place. For what? What could you possibly take that I wouldn't give you? There is nothing in that safe but life insurance policies. And what the heck do you want with my work files? There is nothing in those. Oh, I see, you're looking for information about the accident. God, man, I told you, you can trust me."

"No. I can't." He dropped the safe and files and pushed past her, almost causing Daphne to fall backward down the steps. I was going to stick it to him for that move, but Stanley beat me to it. The kid swarmed him like an octopus.

All I saw was the kid's fists, feet, knees and elbows tagging Randolph. Neither I nor Daphne moved to intervene. As a matter of fact, we both sat on the bottom step and watched her boy go to work. Whichever direction Randolph turned, there was a punch or a kick waiting for him. The kid beat him down, Randolph was on his knees trying to crawl away when Martin walked up on us.

"This is criminal! You can't beat him like that!"

"No!" Daphne jumped up from the step. "Breaking and entering is criminal. We came home and caught him red-handed with my belongings in tow. My son was protecting our domain. Now get him out of here, Martin, before I call the police!" She stomped her foot on the sidewalk and said, "Get!"

When I stood to strap my pistol back, I became cognizant of the fact that we had drawn attention to ourselves. Some of Daphne's Clark Street neighbors were at their back doors looking out at a spectacle that probably made most of them very uncomfortable: four black people standing over a crawling, crying white man in a suit.

Martin also became aware of the neighbors and tried to help Randolph up, but he kept collapsing and whimpering. It wasn't until Martin whispered that the neighbors might call an ambulance, which would in turn bring the police, did Randolph steady himself. He understood the fact that he was in the wrong. He straightened out enough to walk from the courtyard to his midnight-blue BMW SUV, which was parked in the guest slot.

While Stanley and I were watching Martin and Randolph climb into the SUV, Daphne put her possessions back in the house, retrieved Eleanor's gift from Martha's Vineyard and locked her door. She was ready to roll, and, under the observant eyes of her neighbors, so was I.

"Wow," was all I could say sitting in Eleanor's kitchen. Every countertop, every hanging pan and most of the appliances were stainless steel. Her stove had eight jets, two ovens and a grill. She had a deep fryer just for fish and one for everything else. Her meat freezer was a walk-in, and when Stanley opened the refrigerator door to get himself some water, the vegetable crisper I saw could hold two turkeys.

Stanley, who had been here before, was making himself at home by putting together a ham-and-cheese sandwich. Daphne followed the houseman to where Eleanor was. Supposedly, Eleanor was not dressed to entertain male guests.

The houseman seemed agitated by our arrival. As big as this young brother was, I hoped it wasn't us who had him upset.

Looking at Stanley's ham sandwich reminded me of the appetite of youth. When I was his age I ate exactly like him. I considered myself lucky, it would be a while before Chester started to eat nonstop, but even at four he could put away an order of eight chicken nuggets.

As Stanley was putting the fixings back, we heard an outburst from beyond the kitchen door.

"Michael, please!"

"What! Why did you even let this sell-out-ass bitch in

your house! How long y'all going to play this game! Bitch, get the fuck out of here befo' I break my foot off in yo' phony ass! I'm tired of playing these games, lady. You and my punk-ass brother can play with these fools if you want to, but playtime is over! And if y'all keep playing with these lames, y'all can go down too."

Daphne quickly walked through the kitchen and told us it was time to go. Stanley and I both looked back at the door she came through. Somebody on the other side of it threatened her, and called her a bitch. We both went through the door and ran up to Michael.

Stanley threw the first punch, a looping left hook. Michael blocked it with his right and was about to jab Stanley in the face, except that I caught him square in his own face with two left jabs and a bone-crushing right to the chin, which dropped his big ass. Stanley and I stood over him, stomping his head and kicking him in his upper torso.

"D!" Daphne was yanking me by the back of my shirt. "D!" she screamed at me, forcing me to see her, and with seeing her, I saw the situation. I wrapped my arms around a kicking Stanley and we made an exit through the kitchen.

If the truth was told, once we got back in the car and on the road I felt good. A brother was relaxed. The tension from the past day and a half was gone. Burned off kicking that big dude's ass, but of course I had to come up with a mature way to advise Stanley not to partake in such actions again.

"Daphne, why was he cursing you out?" I asked once we got on the expressway.

"D, I have never felt so much hostility in that home in my life. Everyone in the place is on edge. And that muscle-bound butler of hers is walking around like it's his place. He is a cousin or something who just got out of prison.

Eleanor was trying to tell me something about him when he just broke into our conversation. She's scared of him, so she didn't say anything to him. I told him he was being rude and then he just lost it and started cursing me out. But some of the things he said makes me wonder . . ."

"Wonder?"

"Yes, makes me wonder how secret the secret is. Eleanor wasn't cold, but she wasn't herself either. She was guarded toward me even before that big buffoon showed his ass. If she finds the secret out before I tell her, she'll never forgive me."

Once we got to my home I asked Stanley to feed the dogs and let them outside. Daphne went straight upstairs to my bedroom. I followed, and she dropped listlessly on my bed. The pain she felt showed through the lines of anguish that spread across her profile. Looking at her one would think her face had never experienced a smile. Whatever the "it" was, she needed to let it out, before it ate its way out of her. My heart told me to offer comfort, but the vibe I was getting from her told me she wanted to be alone. The clock on my night table read 6:45 PM. Stanley's business had to be taken care of soon.

I went into my bathroom and wet a clean face towel with warm water. It was minor, but I couldn't think of anything else that might comfort her.

I told her Stanley and I were going to get a friend of mine to go with us to pay off his problem. She reached in her purse, pulled out a pen and the check from Martin. She endorsed it and handed it to me without a word said. She rolled under the covers and pulled them over her head, still dressed in her new suit.

When I got downstairs to the kitchen, Stanley was sitting at the table watching the dogs eat. He truly had grown into a lanky kid, long arms and legs. I guessed he was probably five-foot-ten and 140 pounds on a good day. He was at the age where a little weight training could have benefited him greatly. My plans were to take him over to the Y and train him on the free weights after things had settled down. I wanted to show him some basics that he could use for the rest of his life.

"Stanley, don't let the dogs out. Just open the back door so they can use the paper. We're leaving your mama here while we take care of your business."

"That's cool." He didn't move from the table. "You know something Mr. Price?"

I stood in the doorway. "What's that, Stanley?"

"I'm glad my mother broke off my thang with Martin. Yeah, I'm going to miss the loot, but ever since I been hooked up with him Ma been trippin', acting all sad and stuff. At first I thought it was because I was makin' my own cream but it wasn't really the money. It was like whenever she heard me workin' on a deal, she'd just go all flat. Yeah, it was a lot of money, but it wasn't worth seeing her like that.

"Besides, I got two grand in the bank and with what's left from the check I should be able to flip that Aurora. I'm just going to have to go down a little on the rims, but the tint and sound system will be tight, ya can bet that."

"I'm sure they will be, young brother."

"So did Ma start crying?"

"She's settled down some. I'm hoping she takes a nap."

"That ain't gonna happen. Ma don't sleep. It will be one or two in the morning before she falls off, believe me. She makes it hard on a brother trying to make them late-night telephone calls. I don't even bother with the phone after ten. It ain't worth the embarrassment."

"Tell me, Stanley, how did you get the name Snap?"

Guardedly he asked me, “Where did you hear that name?”

“You introduced yourself that way on the phone, when you were talking to your problem.”

“Aw, yeah. When I was a kid I used to get into fights real quick. Other kids started calling me ‘Snap,’ and it stuck.”

“Used to get into fights real quick? Based on what I saw behind your house and out at Eleanor’s you still get into it pretty quick.”

“Today was different, Mr. Price. Both of them dudes tried to disrespect my moms. I had to put in that work.”

He wasn’t bragging; matter of fact, his whole cocky attitude was missing. I walked into the kitchen and placed my hand on his shoulder. “I understand, but, Stanley, if you don’t listen to anything else I tell you, hear this: Think before you do. Ten seconds of thinking could have saved many a man from jail and death. If you give yourself ten seconds before acting, I guarantee you a better life. Trust me on this.”

Truer words I’ve never spoken, but knowing right and doing right is two different things. I try to give myself ten seconds, and more times than not, I do calm down before I react.

“Yeah, Ma tells me that all the time. ‘Think before you do. Think before you speak.’ And I am getting better, Mr. Price, I am. Like I said, I got that name when I was a kid.

“I used to get into fights over kids teasing me about how I smelled. You see my granddaddy would make us—me and moms—eat a piece of garlic and take a spoonful of cod-liver oil every day. And when I would be at school playing, I’d start sweating, and this fishy garlic smell would come out and kids would tease me. And because it was true, I did stink, I would fight them. All a kid had to do was make reference to something stinking. A lot of times it wasn't even me, but I would still snap and start fighting. In fifth grade kids just started calling me 'Snap.'"

All the while he spoke, he continued to look expectantly toward the kitchen doorway. Even though he was no longer speaking of his mother, his solemn tone indicated the worry he felt. Gone was the bravado, what remained was distress. He loved his "moms," but like me, he was uncertain of how to soothe her.

"Let's go. I'm going to get Ricky to ride with us just in case some drama occurs with your problem."

"Your boy Ricky? The guy that owns every liquor store on southside?"

Damn if the kid didn't sound excited, like he was going to meet a celebrity. "I don't know about every liquor store on the southside, but yeah, we going to see that Ricky Brown."

"Wow, should I go home and put on something better?"

"No! Let's ride."

Who did the kid think he was going to meet? Donald Trump? Ricky Brown was nobody. It bugged me that kid got all hyped about meeting Ricky. He wasn't no more important than me; yeah . . . I was player hating.

Going to get Ricky wasn't about securing help. No assistance was required with Stanley's problem. What I needed from my best friend was his opinion on the situation with my son and Regina, and validation that I was thinking right. Despite the changes Ricky had been going through, he remained my sounding board.

My once night-clubbing, gambling, weed-selling, adulterous friend has become settled. The only street-related activity Ricky involved himself in these days was the selling of marijuana, and that's because weed selling for Ricky Brown was a matter of pride. It was no longer a business for him. He had no distribution network or people working under him. He supplied only his lifetime customers. And according to them and him, he found the best weed in the world.

These five guys were more his smoke buddies than customers. Last year he flew all five to Amsterdam for two weeks. Two of the five are now trying to get citizenship there, because of their relaxed laws on marijuana. I didn't go; smoking weed was never really my thing. I preferred to drink and gamble.

Ricky would go gambling if I begged him hard enough. And if he went out drinking, two drinks and he was gone, and he only drank at bars. He wouldn't go anywhere near a club. To quote him: "I ain't gonna end up being da oldest motherfucker in da club."

When Ricky Brown said, "Ain't nothing out here in da streets fo' me, D. I have more fun at home playing' with da kids." I believed him, only because Ricky Brown had already done everything there was to be done on the streets.

The catalyst for Ricky's change, although he would deny it, was the case we'd worked on together six months before. He hired me to protect his sister-in-law. That case changed us all, but he'd never admit it. I'd nicknamed the case "One Dead Preacher."

When we pulled up to Ricky's mini castle, he was sitting on the front porch with his oldest daughter, Tiffany. Ricky and his wife Martha have six children. Tiffany is one hundred percent Martha, more clone than daughter. All she got from Ricky was his name. Her round face, her rich, flawless brown skin and her short curvy stature all came from Martha.

As we walked up the stone steps, Tiffany got up to greet me with a hug and a smile. My best friend remained seated. His eyes were on Stanley.

"Hey, Uncle Da—" She stopped midway through the greeting before I got my hug, and said, "Oh, hold up, I know that ain't Snap coming over my joint. What's up with you, kid!" She turned from me and gave Stanley my hug.

"Hey, Tiff, what are you doing here?"

"I live here!" She moved from him and hugged me briefly and turned her attention back to him.

"You live here? I thought this was Ricky Brown's house."

"Ricky Brown is my daddy."

"Yeah right, I woulda known if Ricky Brown was your pops."

"Some people's business ain't everybody's business. My name is Tiffany Brown, right?" Her hands went to her budding hips.

"Yeah. Wow. I didn't even know."

She sucked her teeth. "You wasn't supposed to know. Enough about that. Snap, I sure hope you been studying your French over the summer. I'm not with carrying you this year." She was no longer smiling.

"Carrying me?" He darted his eyes quickly to me and then Ricky. "You didn't carry me last year. I just copped your notes a couple of times."

"Whatever. You know senior year is too serious to be playing."

"Yeah, yeah, yeah, but later for all that, hear me on this. I'm gonna flip that Aurora this weekend!"

"No!" Tiffany yelped.

"I told y'all last year, I wasn't tryin' to be seventeen years old on the bus."

"You made seventeen?"

"In July."

"And finna get a *caaar*! Daddy! Do you hear this? I told you seventeen is too old to be catching the bus to school.

Daddy, I'm going to be the only seventeen-year-old on the bus. You got to think about it some more." She had turned her pleading eyes to Ricky.

Ricky rose from his seat and beckoned me to follow him. "Good grades first, and then a car. Show me first, baby."

I could tell this was an established point between them because her attention went back to Stanley. I followed Ricky into the house.

"What color are you going to get?" The kids sat on opposite porch ledges, facing each other.

"Gold. And I'm getting Floyd and them to do the tint. I saw the one I'm gettin' over there on Western day before yesterday."

"Gold would look nice. I know May is happy."

"Ain't no guarantee me and May gonna be together this year."

Standing inside the house away from the door and out of their sight, Ricky stopped to eavesdrop, and I did too. I wanted to hear what the kid said about Mitch's daughter.

"Yeah right, May the only good-looking girl that's going to put up with you hanging out with them thugs, you'd better keep her."

"Why you always got to be like that?"

"Like what?"

"All direct and straight to the point."

"Well, I'm just telling you like it is. People judge you by the company you keep, and none of my girls trying to catch a bullet meant for one or your thug friends. Yeah, you cute and all, with that clean cut and bowlegs, and everybody says you dress nice, but you hang around thugs, and thugs be shooting at thugs. May is the only girl I know who thinks you worth the risk."

"Man, you and your girls ain't all that."

"Whatever, that's why every guy at the school been sweatin' us since we were freshmen."

Ricky whispered, "That's my girl," and we walked to the dining room to join Martha, who was sitting on the couch with remote in hand, flipping the plasma screen's channels.

"Sixty-eight dollars a month for cable and there is not a darn thing on." She placed the remote on the white marble coffee table. "Hey, D." I went to her and kissed her on the cheek.

"Hey yourself." I slid next to her on the white leather sofa.

"If you came over for dinner you're in bad shape today. Ricky made a pizza out of sausage links, worst mess I ever tasted in my life." Even though Martha was in her housecoat, I could tell she'd worked today. Her watch, wedding ring, diamond tennis bracelet and stockings lingered from her workday.

Ricky started a small cleaning business about fifteen years ago, and under Martha's watchful eye it had grown into the city's second-largest office cleaning company. Last year he turned all operations over to her. He kept himself busy with his rental properties and liquor stores.

"Links, bro?" I asked Ricky.

"Seemed like a good idea at the time, but Martha's right, it's a mess. I got some shrimp coming from Whites if you hungry." He dropped down to the rocker recliner next to the couch. The Browns had converted their formal dining room into a very cozy family room equipped with three computers, a foosball game, an overstuffed love seat and a surround-sound system. There was also a game table used for dominos, chess and backgammon, and all the Browns played competitively.

"You ordered shrimp?"

"Yeah, I had to get something. Your daughter wouldn't touch da pizza."

"Where the rest of the kids?" I asked.

"The boys are at dance and the girls are at karate."

"Huh?"

Ricky and Martha chuckled, "It does sound backwards, don't it? But that's how it is. The boys are taking tap dance lessons and the twins are taking karate. You should see Monique and Monica in their karate suits. 'Double trouble' is what their sensei calls them."

"I would like to see that. How soon before they come in?"

"Tiffany should be leaving to get them in a few; they're right up the street, the South Shore Cultural Center has summer activities."

"Well maybe I'll see them when I get back. I came to get Ricky to ride with me down to 47th Street."

A big grin appeared on his face.

"Lord yes, get him out of here, I never thought I'd say that, but he needs to go out."

"Martha!" He sat up in the recliner.

"Baby, I'm sorry, but you need some air and something to do. Being in the house is not for everybody."

"Sound like you sayin' you sick of me."

"I didn't say that, I simply said you need something to do. You haven't been doing house things all these years. I see no sense in starting now."

Looking past Martha, a noticeable darker patch in the wall grabbed my attention. The wall was eggshell white, but the patch was almost yellow. Seeing a patch in Martha's wall was unusual. Her home had been flawless for years. Ricky's businesses had been doing well for years, and her home reflected that. Martha bought the best and she bought frequently. A patch in her wall was out of the norm.

"What happened to the wall?" I thought it was an innocent enough question.

Martha's attention went to the television. Ricky, who had stood from the recliner looked down to the polished floorboards.

"The wall y'all, what happened?"

"Nothin', da boys just knocked a little hole in it and I fixed it."

I got up and walked over to it. "You fixed it, huh?"

"Yeah, I fixed it," he said, pulling up his pants.

"He fixed it, just like he fixed the refrigerator that's still leaking, the ceiling fan he taped up, the doorknob he nailed, and let's not forget the floor tiles he fixed with Krazy Glue."

Ricky took his straw hat from atop one of the computers. "Let's go man."

"Hold up a second, you fixed a door knob with a nail?"

The tips of his ears were turning red. "If you want me to ride with you, let's go man."

"Awight, awight," I said restraining a laugh. "Hey man can you cash a check for thirteen grand?"

He looked to his wife, "Martha?"

Something on television had her attention; she answered without looking up, "Yes, the receipts from the stores on 51st Street didn't get dropped."

I followed Ricky down to the basement. I saw more of his handiwork on the stairway railing. It had been taped into the brackets with duct tape. "Man, I can fix this railing for you."

"It's fixed."

"Okay."

He pulled thirteen grand from his walk-in safe and cashed the check. The previous owner of Ricky's mini castle home had had the safe installed. I believe it was one of the main reasons they bought the house. I peeled seven grand from the bundle of bills Ricky handed me.

"I got a couple of Time-Life books on home maintenance. You can borrow them anytime you want."

"Look-a-here man, obviously I ain't no handyman, but I tried, awight? It was just somethin' to do."

"All I'm saying, Ricky, is we can do the repairs together, me, you and the books, cause I can't fix everything either."

"You do awight. You can fix most thangs."

"But I use the books, Ricky. What I'm saying is I can show what I know, and the books can do the rest."

"Man, look-a-here, I'm-a get somebody in here and fix those thangs. Awight, I had a little time on my hands so I tried to do a little somethin'. I don't need ya mister-fix-it books."

"Cool. I was just letting you know I had them."

"I don't need 'em . . . Now what's up with 47th Street, you goin' to get a new brim?" He took a pistol from a shelf inside the safe and pushed the heavy door closed.

"Nope, the kid upstairs is Daphne's son, she hired me to help him pay off a debt."

"Daphne?"

"She used to live across the alley from me in Harvey."

"Oh yeah, I seen her, Regina and Regina's mama together at something Martha had me go to. That girl now grown up! That's her boy huh? Is that the same li'l fellah that used to keep a pocketful of bottle tops, bones and nails and thangs?"

I chuckled, "Yeah, that was him. And there is something else going on with Daphne too, man, some other threat, but she hasn't felt the need to tell me about it yet. A guy in a white Bentley pulled alongside us and cursed her out. She acted like it was nothing, but something is up. The same is true with her rich friend out in Olympia Fields; we go out there and the butler all but pimp-slaps her."

"No shit. Well you know how womens is, D; they don't never you tell the whole story until they have to. But I remember dat li'l chubby scamp of a boy though. He was always under your feet. Dat's somthin', dat li'l ole round kid now grew straight up. I thought he was gonna be fat. Umh. Let's ride, partner." He dropped the .38 into his sweatsuit jacket pocket without a second thought.

When we walked into McDonald's, Stanley's problem was there with three of his crew. They were boys, none over twenty-one. Young prison apprentices who could easily become young productive members of society if given an ounce of encouragement. Their leader, James Taylor, also known as JT, damn near gagged when he saw Ricky and me walk in.

He greeted us with, "Damn Snap, you said they was your uncles, but I thought you was bullshittin'. "

After Stanley paid him, JT asked Ricky did he have any openings at his stores. "Because I'm really gettin' tired of being out here like this and I hear you got a program for cats like me."

At one time, young men who worked for Ricky sold weed from his hot dog carts. The guys who were industrious and made their quotas moved up to management and got to oversee other hot dog carts. If they proved good managers, Ricky brought them into his legitimate liquor-store business.

These street-recruited managers are largely responsible for the phenomenal growth of Ricky's liquor stores. What he had done to continue getting young goal-orientated brothers to work for him, since he no longer dabbled in street distribution, was start a management training program with his handpicked street managers doing the training.

Ricky told JT yes, he had a program for young cats looking to go straight, but to qualify a cat had to be either in high school, taking GED classes or in college. The program paid a management trainee eleven dollars and twenty-five cents an hour.

A trainee worked three point five hours and got paid for eight, as long as he was enrolled in school or a GED program. The boys quickly calculated that to be $400 a week, after taxes.

Of the boys sitting at the table, JT and Stanley were the only two in high school; the others were high-school dropouts. Stanley and JT wanted to know what they had to do next. Ricky told them to call him when school started, and if they were enrolled, they could apply to his program.

To the dropouts, he gave phone numbers to libraries where he knew the GED instructors. He told them if they provided letters of their enrollment, they could apply to his program as well. He gave each boy sitting at the table his business card.

I was a hundred percent sure Ricky would let all these kids into his program if they called. These were the kind of kids he bent over backwards for, those with desire, but no direction. His dominant interest however, was in the leader. JT was the diamond in the rough Ricky would refine. It was boys like him with the natural ability to lead who expanded Ricky's liquor-store empire.

Driving Ricky home and dropping him off, I found it curious how being in the company of the right person at the right time could provide the level-headedness that's needed. Seeing Ricky with those boys, feeling his concern, and sensing how badly he wanted to guide them down a better path was all the confirmation I needed.

My head was on right. Chester having my name was more important than him having Peal's money. My name would provide him with identity, money wouldn't. Fighting Regina on this was the right thing to do. She was wrong. I was right.

When we pulled to my house I noticed a white Bentley parked across the street. Instead of going into the underground garage, I made the block and came back around on the west side. I parked three cars behind with my lights out. And Stanley and I watched a big guy getting out of the Bentley from the driver's side. He was holding something in his hand. I drew both .9mms and told Stanley to stay put. I slipped out my Caddy and was about four steps behind the guy, who was a step away from my porch, when someone from across the street yelled, "MacKnock, watch out!" and opened fire on me from the Bentley. I dove to the grass, rolling. The big guy followed me, shooting down into the grass all around me. I stopped moving because maybe he was not trying to shoot me and I didn't want to roll into a bullet.

I guessed right because he stopped shooting and darted across the street into the Bentley. They pealed out from the curb. Stanley ran to me, "Are you okay, Mr. Price?" He helped me up and patted me for wounds. "I can't believe he missed standing over you like that!"

"He wasn't trying to shoot me. He was trying to stop me from seeing him. Let's get inside before the police roll up. If they don't see us standing out front, they will ride on by. Let's get in."

"Did you see him?"

"Nothing but his feet and the fire from his pistol."

Shots fired are not a rarity on my block. Mostly it's teenagers popping off rounds in an alley. With us not standing outside, I hoped the police would assume that was what occurred and roll on by. I didn't feel like talking to them or filing a report.

# Chapter Eleven

When Stanley and I walked into my house, Daphne was sitting on the sofa. She greeted us with a tense, nervous smile. I thought she was upset about the shots, but that wasn't the case.

"All done?" she asked us.

"Huh?"

"With Stanley's situation?"

"Oh yeah, that problem is solved," I told her.

"Hey Ma, check this, this dude tried to bust a ca—"

Daphne cut him off with, "Tell me on the ride home, son."

"Y'all leaving?" I asked surprised.

"Yes, I think it would best . . . While you were gone . . . Regina called. I was dozing. The phone was ringing and I answered it. She was surprised I was here. Even more surprised that I was here and you weren't. We talked . . . One thing led to another . . . She said Randolph called her and told her I was representing you . . . She's pissed about it . . . called me some names . . . I called her some names, and she now knows that we were intimate." She ran the last words together as she stood from the sofa.

Her eyes were on me and she was holding her breath.

"And what does that have to do with you leaving tonight?" I asked.

"I didn't know if you would want me to stay or not? And Regina said some things that made me uncomfortable."

Stanley stood there looking at us like we were the television.

"You know what, we need to talk alone. Would you excuse us, Stanley? I got half a pizza from Nancy's Space Age on the bottom shelf of the fridge."

"Cool." He dashed to the kitchen.

With the kid gone, I stood right up on her and asked, "Now what were you saying?"

"Regina's statements upset me. And you and I hadn't talked about how we were going to handle things with her. So I figured we both could use a little space."

"Oh . . . okay . . . But did I tell you that I really liked you in that camisole?" I lowered my head to her neck and kissed it, again and again.

"What?"

"I like your suit, too." I kissed her neck on the other side. "I like how you matched your colors with mine." I kissed the tip of her ear. "I like your thin but shapely legs." I kissed her ear lobe. "I like your pouty lips and round hips." I lightly kissed her lips and the tip of her nose. "I like your thin hair and slender neck." I unbuttoned her jacket.

"And in case you forgot, we got someplace to go tonight." My hand was under her camisole; I flipped my thumb across her nipple and kissed the top of her cleavage. "I need to go there. It's been a hard day and I hear people can relax there." I dropped my hand to her thighs and found her stockings were off. I took my hand up and found wetness. "Mm, you can't leave here, woman . . . no . . . you got to take me to the country."

Later, I planned to ask her about the white Bentley, but at that moment my mind was on convincing her to spend the night.

It was twelve-thirty AM and the phone was blaring. Daphne grabbed it and said, "hello" and then, "sorry." She handed the receiver to me.

It was Regina. Before a word came out of my mouth, she called me an evil conniving bastard. She said she hoped Daphne was a good fuck and a good lawyer, because it would be a cold day in hell before I saw Chester again. She advised me to forget I had a son.

It was officially on.

Neither Daphne nor I could go back to sleep after Regina's call. She laid with her head on my chest, not saying a word for close to half an hour before she asked, "What do you think?"

"About?"

"Regina."

"I think she's being the spoiled brat she has always been."

"Only a man would say that."

"What, is this another one of Gina's power moves?"

"I didn't say that, but I do understand how she feels. I'm her girl and I'm laying up with her man."

"I am not her man. I am her ex-husband. It's been over between me and Regina." I was lying a little, but technically it was the truth.

"Regardless, I understand how she feels."

The doorbell chimed, and Yin and Yang went ballistic. The only time they bark at the doorbell is when Ricky rings it. I looked at the clock. It was close to one in the morning, no longer Ricky's traveling time. A bit spooked, I immediately went to the door.

When I opened the door, the words out his mouth were, "Man, what the fuck did you do to Gina? Martha had to go out to her place to stop her from comin' over here and shootin' ya ass. What da fuck is up?"

What stopped him from barreling past me into the house was Yin and Yang. They would not allow him to pass the doorway. Their ears were lowered and their teeth were bared. Ricky must have done something really mean to them when they were puppies, because they truly hate him.

"Man, you better tell these mutts to bow down, before I put they ass to sleep fo' real." To them, he said, "You two mutts ain't scaring me." But he didn't move past the break of the doorway. I gave the command "friend" and they reluctantly let him pass.

"Martha went out to Harvey this time of night?"

"Yeah, and you lucky she did." Ricky dropped his heavy frame down on my couch. "Gina was set on comin' over here with pistol cocked. What's going on, man?"

"I was going to tell you earlier, but I didn't. Regina is getting married to this rich white cat and she wants him to adopt Chester?"

"What? A white cat? Damn, pissed you off, huh? But hold it, how she gonna put a boy up fo' adoption dat got a daddy?"

"That's what I said."

"It can happen." Daphne walked into the front room in my robe.

Ricky turned his melon-sized head to see who was speaking. She walked into his line of vision, "Hello, I'm Daphne Nelson."

"Mm . . . oh!" The eyebrows on his fat face rose with his exclamation. Ricky's huge face shows what he feels and thinks. "You must be 'the heifer that's over there now' dat Regina wants to come see." Ricky alone laughed at his Regina rendition. "You ain't got to introduce yaself like we strangers. I knew you when you used to jump rope out in Harvey." Ricky turned his melon to me. "And you did too, didn't you? You said you was protecting her son. Is da boy even here?"

I stepped to him in a snap. "Nigga, who is questioning like that? This is my damn house." Ricky knew good and well he never saw Daphne jumping rope on the block. She had to be a teenager when Regina and I moved to Harvey. Her son was four or five when I first met him.

"I know whose house it is, man. Calm yourself." He put a sly, consoling grin on his face. "I was just tryin' to get my facts straight. I come over and she got on ya robe, you in ya shorts and ya wife—"

"Ex-wife!" I interjected.

"Okay, ya ex-wife, Gina, screamin' on da phone about shootin' you and a heifer. I was trying' to get a under-standin' of what was really goin' on. But shit, I didn't even have to come over here. I coulda stayed my fat ass in da bed." He turned away from me and Daphne and huffed. "I don't need dis here, call myself helpin'. I ain't da one dat got the li'l girl from down the block in my bed. No wonder Gina talkin' about comin' over and bustin' a cap in ya ass."

Before I could set his self-righteous tail straight, the doorbell chimed and all three of us jumped. Ricky asked, "You think I should get it? It might be her."

"No, this my house, and I can answer the door."

I went to the door and asked, "Who is it?"

"It's me, David. Carol."

I thought I even heard the dogs sigh in relief. Out the

corner of my eye I caught a flicker of Daphne running up the stairs. My guess was to get dressed. I commanded the dogs to the kitchen and let Carol in.

"David, I'm sorry to bother you like this. It's just that I got a call from Regina a little while ago and it bothered me." Carol walked in and hugged me. "Are you all right?"

"Yeah, I'm fine. Come on in, Ricky's here too."

"Hey, Carol the kitty." Ricky had twisted his melon all the way around to see Carol. They have a history. He flirts with her, she can't stand the sight of him. "Come on over here and sit next to me."

"Thank you, but no thank you, Mr. Brown."

When she walked past the couch Ricky moaned, "Slimmie slimmie, please let me."

Carol sucked her teeth and slightly audibly said, "Disgusting, married, yellow pig."

I know he heard her, but he acted like he didn't, and after she sat in the recliner she smiled at him just as nice and asked, "How is Mrs. Brown?"

"She fine . . . Dat sho' is a pretty sundress. Dat African print looks nice on you. Did you go to Africa to get it?"

Carol completely ignored his compliment and question, "David, Regina was livid. I had the office phone forwarded to my home, and the message she left you was serious. She's planning on going to court over your son. Whatever plans you have, you better get started right away.

"She left another message by mistake; I think she thought she'd reached her attorney's service. She was giving him the go-ahead to get started. What happened?"

I hunched my shoulders and threw up my hands. "I guess her lawyer boyfriend called her and told her Daphne was my lawyer, is the best I can figure."

"And that sent her into a rage? No. That doesn't sound

like Regina." Carol sat back in the big chair and crossed her legs.

Ricky reached into the pocket of his sweatsuit jacket and pulled out a pack of Newports and lit one.

"Yeah you right 'bout dat. Sounds like somebody ain't tellin' you everthang. Huh?"

"Pardon?"

"Don't pay him any attention, Carol."

Daphne hadn't left to change clothes. She returned wearing my robe and carrying the file of newspapers from her trunk.

"Oh! Hello, Daphne." Carol gave Daphne the same smile she gave Ricky and settled her catlike eyes on me.

I sat down on the couch next to Ricky and Daphne sat in the love seat. Carol, who was in the recliner, was kind of out of our circle.

"Well, ain't this cozy?" Ricky exhaled smoke and words simultaneously.

Daphne was directly across from Ricky and me with my mahogany coffee table between us. She placed the file on the table and emptied the contents. Carol stood and walked toward us.

Daphne's eyes went to the newspapers on the table, then up to us. Her eyes were filled with tears. Her hands and shoulders started trembling. I was going to go to her, but Carol sat down and hugged her. Ricky tore off the top of his box of Newports and extinguished his cigarette in it.

Daphne cried openly. "I didn't mean for it to happen." She pulled free from Carol's hug and pointed to the papers. "Look . . . look and see what I did. I did that. I got those people killed!"

The headlines read, CHURCH BUS CRASHES. 16 BURN TO DEATH.

"I set the accident up. The driver of the car was a pro. He was supposed to get a truck to rear-end him up on the embankment, but the car hit the bus and the bus hit the wall. The bus blew up and killed all those people. All those church folks burned to death."

Daphne stood and went to my book case/bar. She filled a highball glass full of Remy and drank. "I told Randolph we had to go to the police." She sipped from the glass. "He said no; told me the case would be our breakthrough case. He represented the families of the passengers on the bus." She looked into her drink. "He was right. It was our breakthrough case.

"After he got all those families large settlements, we became the personal-injury lawyers for black folks. He said he was going to stop doing the staged accidents, but he didn't, and neither did I. The money was too easy. Companies started settling as soon as they saw his name on the documents. Instead of doing fewer staged accidents, we did more."

Holding one of the newspapers in my hand, I said, "I remember this."

"Yeah, me too. Aspire Trucking. The guy who ran the joint was a decent guy. Matthew MacNard was his name. It was a operation with only two trucks. Da accident closed them down."

"Yeah, I remember, the manger of the trucking company shot himself in the head."

"David!" Carol shot me a look.

"What!"

Carol cut her eyes to Daphne. I hadn't thought about how my words might have added to her guilt.

"Damn, baby, I'm sorry, but this wasn't your fault. Death goes where it's supposed to. You, me, nobody can direct it. God's will is God's will."

This was a painful lesson for me to learn, but I had learned. We are powerless over death.

"Try telling that to Eleanor. Her mother was on the bus. My girlfriend's mother was killed in an accident I set up!"

Ricky adjusted his mass on the sofa and said, "You didn't put her mama on dat bus and you wasn't drivin' da car dat hit da bus. Yeah, settin' up da accident was fucked up, but like D said, you ain't God.

"It was a bad time fo' the whole city, li'l girl; everybody had somebody on dat bus. Seems like the funerals lasted fo'ever. Da whole thang was sad."

"Daphne, I agree with them, and I think your friend Eleanor would too."

"I don't know. If it was me and Eleanor had set up an accident that got my mother killed, I would want her." She poured more Remy and drank without looking up. "Randolph married Eleanor after the accident. He married her and bought her a mansion out in the 'burbs, all out of guilt, I believe. The marriage didn't last long, but she got to keep the mansion."

Daphne returned to her seat next to Carol and gathered the papers. We all sat there quietly until Carol said, "Not meaning to be insensitive, but how will this help David with his son?"

Daphne answered, "Leverage against Randolph. We can always threaten to go public." She pulled a thin manila envelope from the hanging file. "David, this is the only paper trail leading from the driver of the car to Randolph. Here you have copies of checks written to him for previous accidents, along with invoices from his hospital stays and a memo telling me to order plane tickets for him to Barbados. The only people who can connect the driver to Randolph are Eleanor and me."

"Eleanor?" Carol asked.

"Yes. She used to bird-dog for Randolph. Started out doing only data entry, but once she found out about bird-dogging and the commissions associated with it, she out-did me. Eleanor takes money very seriously.

"She knew the driver in the accident. If she had seen his name associated with her mother's death, she would have known Randolph was involved. He had me remove all this information from the office records." She fanned through the folder. "I thought he believed I destroyed the info, but catching him searching my home causes me to think otherwise. I want you to keep this for me, David." She tossed the file into my lap.

The door chimes sounded again. No one moved. We four sat still.

"Answer the door, David," Carol prompted. I waited to see if Ricky was going to say he would get it. I looked at my Rolex—it was a little past two in the morning. When neither Ricky nor anyone else volunteered to answer the door, I got it.

When the front door opened, I experienced an array of emotions; happiness, shock, anger and happiness again. The first face I saw was Martha's, and I was relieved, but behind her I saw Regina and she had the nerve to be smiling. When I looked down at her hand, Chester was holding it, and he looked up at me grinning just as bright-eyed and bushy-headed as he wanted to be and said, "Hey, Daddy Man, we went to White Castle's!" I scooped him up in my arms, and all was right with the world.

Chester didn't stay awake for five minutes. I carried him to the room Stanley was in, but the Stanley slept too bad; he was all over the bed and snored like a drunken old man. I toted my son upstairs to my bed.

I was in no hurry to get back downstairs. Lingering at

the top of the stairs, I listened to see if conversation had started. It had, but I couldn't tell if it was Martha or Carol who prompted Daphne to retell her story. I took a couple of steps down and heard Daphne begin.

"I physically cannot go over it all again, but I will tell you this. Randolph is not a man to be trusted. He was a party in the death of his first wife's mother, and he has kept the truth from her and others who deserve to know what happened to their loved ones. He is a man solely motivated by wealth. I think it would be a mistake to allow a man like him into your little boy's life."

The second Daphne finished, Regina launched, "Who I let into my son's life is absolutely none of your concern!" The harshness with which Regina spoke brought me down the stairs.

Regina's index finger was targeted at Daphne's heart. "And if not for Martha, your concern would have been to get whatever legal expertise you possess in order. Because, missy, you were going to court!"

When I entered the living area, Regina was sitting on the tip of the sofa cushion between Martha and Ricky. Across the coffee table were Daphne and Carol. Regina's eyes were locked on Daphne. Daphne, along with Martha and Ricky, looked at me expectantly.

I asked Regina, "Has Martha changed your mind about going to court?"

She rolled her emerald eyes from Daphne, cast them sharply on me and said, "Yes, she has. I was wrong, David. Chester is your son and he should bear your name. We were blessed, David, to have good friendships that survived after our marriage. I thank God for Martha, and you should too."

I stood there looking at the austere expression on my ex-wife's face. There was no remorse. She matter-of-factly admitted that she was wrong, and that was all I was going to get. The past twenty-four hours of agitation caused by her were to be forgotten.

Martha on the other hand, had a warm, happy, grateful smile on her round face, and that pulled the "thank you" from me to Regina.

"No need to thank me. As Martha pointed out, it was the Christian thing to do," was Regina's reply.

A slight revelation noticeably crossed Carol's face. She jerked her head toward Daphne and said "Well, I guess that means David won't be needing your *legal* services after all."

Although my eyes saw both women smiling at each other, it wasn't a pleasant feeling that generated from the love seat.

"Yes, you're right," Daphne said, standing.

She walked over to me and laid her hand on my chest. She let my robe fall open, allowing only me to see her nakedness, but everyone in the room could tell it had fallen open. She looked over her shoulder to Carol and Regina and said, "David is a bachelor, a free and available black man, and, ladies, I am interested. If you had him and didn't keep him, too bad. If you wanted him and didn't move on him, too bad. I'm here now. I'm leaving tonight only because my son has a 7 AM dentist appointment. If not for that, ladies, I would be camped out."

The next sound heard in the room was her lips smacking on mine. She then shook her booty at those sitting in the living area and dashed up the stairs, giggling.

Damn! I was feeling that girl.

Daphne and Stanley were the first to leave. If I didn't know any better, I'd think Martha, Carol and Regina made it up in their minds that they weren't leaving with her in my home. After her little living-room dance, which only Ricky and me found funny, the other women glued themselves to their seats.

Daphne got dressed, woke up Stanley, kissed me goodbye again and left. No sooner had the door closed, than I got the sucking teeth, the exasperation, the popping of lips, and a whispered, "How could he? She's got to be fifteen years younger."

When I turned around from the door, I couldn't tell which of the three said what, because they all smiled at me pleasantly.

I'd decided to ignore them all and go warm up some food, but gunshots rang out and we all froze.

Yin and Yang moved first. They bolted from the kitchen to my side. I told everyone to remain still, because if they moved the dogs would strike. Gunshots fired as close as those puts them in attack mode. I opened the front door and directed them to "secure."

Their constant barking and growling let me know the area was occupied. My intention was to go upstairs and get my pistols, but when I turned, Ricky was there and handed me his.

I wasn't ready for outside.

Seeing their bodies sprawled across my steps broke me down to my knees. I crawled to them. There was nothing to be done. I did no service checking for a pulse or trying to stop the flow of blood from their heads and chests. Mouth-to-mouth resuscitation did nothing. The mother and son were dead.

Wednesday morning found me alone sitting at my grandmother's kitchen table cleaning pistols. I hadn't slept. I called Ricky and asked him to go to Peal's office with me. He reminded me of the early-morning plan he, Regina and I came up with.

Daphne's information was to be given to Eleanor. The plan didn't seem enough to me. More was needed. Ricky disagreed and told me to get some sleep. He was wrong. Cleaning the pistols had me on the right track. What was needed had to do with the pistols. It must have, because holding my pistols made me feel better.

Ricky called me back and tried to make me swear I wouldn't go over to the lawyer's office. I hung up the phone. Attorney Peal needed to see me.

I am not really a violent man. Putting my pistol to Attorney Peal's head, or any other man's head, is not how I operate. It was his condescending, arrogant, superior attitude that drew my pistol from the holster to his head. It was the way he pointed to the chair in front of his desk and said, "Sit down right there and be brief, my time concerning this matter is limited." I didn't take the seat he ordered me to.

Instead I slammed his office door closed, and got with his ass. He tried to run past me, but I clotheslined him. His head was between my forearm and bicep; I tried to stop his screaming by choking him, but he started biting my arm. That's when I put the pistol to his head and pulled him to the floor. Thank God Ricky came in when he did. His dragging me from that office saved my life and Peal's life. Hopefully I will do better with Eleanor.

# BOOK TWO

# Chapter Twelve

"Once you go black, you never go back." I heard the saying decades ago when I was in college; some white girls who came to one of our frat parties were giggling it in a corner. With Attorney Randolph Peal it appeared to be the truth.

His first wife, Eleanor, is an African-American woman. They had no children together, but judging by the size of her Olympia Fields estate, she did quite well in the divorce. Waiting at the black cast-iron gates, the only opening to the solid red-brick wall that surrounds her estate, I sit fumbling with the words I am to say to her.

This is not an easy task for me, causing someone else pain for my own gain, but it must be done; Peal has left me no other choice. I hear her houseman announcing my arrival over the intercom buzz. The gates roll open, and I drive up the long maple- and oak-tree-lined path to the estate.

Wealth, as it is meant to do, intimidates me. Seeing and feeling the ostentatiousness of the property lessens my own personal worth. Even though I am riding in a 2003 DTS, I feel minor, like a peon. Yes, I am okay with money, but being okay ain't being wealthy. Peal can afford to lose this property in a divorce and continue to live downtown and build out in the high-brow suburb of Lake Forest.

I park my Caddy at the end of the *U* in front of the estate. I grab the folder with the information Daphne gathered. Walking through the bright, near-blinding sunlight toward the home, I pat my shirt pocket for my sunglasses, but they are missing. My mind goes back to the struggle with Peal. They probably came undone from my pocket then. I give myself a quick once-over, Rocawear blue jeans, a white short-sleeved shirt and new all-white Reeboks. I look all right.

At the foot of the Colonial-style mansion, I take four steps up and walk between two thirty-foot white pillars to the fifteen-foot wooden door. I don't have to ring or knock. The houseman opens the colossal door and greets me with a smile. I see big lumps under both his eyes. If he can smile at me after the whipping Stanley and I gave him, I certainly can smile at him.

He doesn't look at all like the butler type. He's about six feet five inches tall and an easy 300 pounds of solid muscle. He answers the door in a sleeveless T-shirt and baggy blue-jean shorts. On his left shoulder is the tattooed number three and the capital letter M; on his right shoulder are three capitol M's in a row. My guess is that the houseman is in his late twenties, and the young tank of a brother could probably bench-press 400 pounds, but he's kind of slow with his dukes—after all an "old hat" like me was able to sting him with jabs and a bone-crusher.

"She'll meet you in the library, Mr. Price."

"You can call me David, bro."

With a standard greeting smile still on his face he answers, “Naw, Mr. Price. I cain’t do that. Ms. Peal told all of us to address everybody as Mr. and Ms. No disrespect meant. It’s about keeping my cheddar job,” he pauses to look me square in the eye. I’m thinking he’s about to get froggy, but with a smile still on his face he winks and leans a little toward my ear and says in a real low tone, “And believe what I tell you, boss, this is a cheddar job. You might want to think about a career change, since your clients be gettin’ gunned down and all.” He is grinning now, and he stands straight.

“This way, sir,” he says and walks away from me.

I yank the pistol on my left free with my right hand. I run up on him and jab the pistol into back of his head. “You don’t want to say nothing like that to me ever again.” He stops walking.

“You ain’t gonna shoot me in here old man, so why you even pull ya gat? Put it away, pops, befo’, you hurt yaself. We’ll get a chance to dance later. I promise.” And he walks on like I didn’t even put a pistol to his head.

One, two, three . . .

Fuck it.

I run up behind and knock him upside the head with the butt of my 9mm. I hit him so hard pain shoots through the small of my back. He falls to his knees. I tell him “I’m not the one to play with, motherfucker,” while I shove the barrel of the pistol into his ear. “You see what I think about putting a slug in you ain’t shit. And if I find out you drive a white Bentley, one of these slugs in this pistol here got your on name it. Now get your stank ass up.” I let him up, but keep my pistol drawn.

I follow him to a room large enough to be a small town’s library.

“Wait in here. Lady will be with you shortly.”

He’s rubbing the knot I just put upside his head, but

the bastard is still grinning. Why, I don't know. Maybe he's just stupid as a mule. Once he left the room I holster my pistol, but I don't snap the strap. People are making me into a violent man. I am not violent. Taking long, deep, cleansing breaths is working. My heart is no longer pounding in my head.

Looking around, I notice none of the book cases in the library are over seven feet high, but they cover the width of all four walls. Three rows of the book cases run down the middle of the floor area. The ceiling and what can be seen of the walls are all stark white. The floor is tiled in a black-and-white checkerboard pattern.

When I look closer at the book cases, I notice they are made of either plastic or vinyl; not wood. There is one black leather captain's chair on wheels and one long white marble table in front of the three rows. There is nothing inviting about the room, no warmth. I'm standing here wondering why a person would make a home library so cold.

Eleanor has entered the library behind me, I turn to greet her and see the sadness. "Who would do such thing, kill her and her son . . . it's so wrong, Mr. Price, so, very, very wrong. When I heard her name on the news I collapsed, I couldn't believe it. Only an evil person would kill a mother and her child."

"I agree, and I will do my best to track the murderer down. Rest assured in knowing that."

"Good, and be swift with your judgment."

The icy tone of her statement surprises me. She grabs me by the hand and is leading me out of the library.

What I have heard about Eleanor I like. The talk about her is all good. People say that her friends and close family live and work on the estate with her. When she made it, she took her circle with her. Her aunt, who cooked for a hotel, now gets paid well to cook for their family. Her uncle, a cab driver, now drives only her. And after two years, the estate continues to be one of the better-looking properties in the area. She knew she needed help to run the estate, and she went to her family and friends and got it.

"Let's walk through the garden, David. We can chat outside." The houseman is standing by the door. "Michael, if it's not too much trouble, could you fix us a little lemonade and bring it out to the gazebo?"

"No problem, it will be ready in a minute. Would you like it made with sparkling water?"

"Oh yes, that would be marvelous. Thank you, Michael."

Out the fifteen-foot door and down the four steps and back into the harsh bullying sun, we take a rocky walkway around the back of the home.

"You know, David, I haven't seen you since my parents' wedding. Oh, you were quite the stepper then: I along with every other woman there couldn't help but watch you dance. Do you still step?"

I did dance quite a bit that day; it was a steppers crowd. Her parents are of my generation, and they and their friends step. Everyone who could, did. And everyone considered themselves a "boss stepper" but only a few really are. Since it was a neighborhood function and would be talked about for months, people were really trying to show off, myself included.

"Not too much at clubs anymore, but I still cut up a bit at weddings and parties."

"Well you were certainly something to watch that day. Be mindful of the path, the rocks can trip you."

The rocks have been laid very well, the path of cobblestones are as even as a sidewalk.

"Randolph's mother started the garden, but I maintained and enlarged it after she left. On hot days like this it smells heavenly. I'm showing off, in case you didn't know. Since the garden club out here ignored my request for membership, I don't really get a chance to show it off much. It took a lot of work to get it right. It's what's called a four-season garden; I have blooms year around. Do you garden?"

"Not flowers. I grow a few collards, peppers and tomatoes, nothing really pretty."

"I would imagine a vegetable garden is just as relaxing."

I never thought about my garden that way, but she is right. Since I hadn't been working on cars lately, it is my garden that has been relaxing me. Four days ago I'd pulled every weed in sight, shifted the soil and built up around the tomatoes and peppers. My tomatoes were doing darn good, and they were doing well without chemical boosters. I'm looking forward to working in it with Chester. Kids like playing in the dirt; at least I did when I was his age.

"Yeah you're right, gardening does relax me."

Eleanor is not a magazine beauty. Her face isn't narrow, nor are her features chiseled. She doesn't possess the strong African look that is so popular as of late. There is nothing exotic about her. Her skin is paper-bag brown. Her forehead is large, her lips are thick, her nose is wide and her eyes are as round as quarters. Her left earlobe is split. Faint old scars can be seen on her neck and left cheek. Pockmarks are on her face, and through her straight weave I can see that her kitchen needs a little work.

She is wearing a pair of khaki cut-offs, yellow leather sandals and a tan Danskin top. Her legs are thick, bowed and hairless. Her toes and fingernails have been done with small daisies painted on each. She is what men back in the day called "stacked": large breasts, thin waist, full hips and a round butt, all this on about a five-foot, eight-inch frame. I imagine Randolph wasn't happy about leaving *all this* woman—at least I wouldn't have been.

I look around the estate and notice all of the landscaping is wonderful, grass cut and edged to perfection, shrubs and trees trimmed and pruned to a *Better Homes and Gardens* exactness. Nothing is out of place or in disorder, but the flower garden is exceptional.

The garden is filled with lilies, magnolias, roses, huge daisies, ferns, morning glories, wild flowers, colorful cabbages, forget-me-nots, cacti, wood chips, pretty rocks, white sand and red clay. It is breathtaking. "Wow," is all I can say. The aroma is glorious. It tickles my nose and forces me to smile. A much-needed calm falls over me standing amid such pungent sweetness. I want to drop down to my knees and bury my nose in the bundles of flowers. I don't. Instead I look to the "'round-the-way-girl" who created this slice of Eden.

"You did this?"

"Yes, ninety five percent of it is mine. Surprised?"

"Honestly, yeah I am."

"Well you aren't the first person we've surprised, and I'm certain you won't be the last. Do you like it?"

"Oh yeah, it's calming in an almost spiritual way."

"Mm, I never looked it as spiritual, simply relaxing. Come sit with me."

I follow along the path. The gazebo is in the middle of the garden. Standing on the steps, I can see the circular pattern of the rows she laid. The roses are the closest to the gazebo.

"I like the circle pattern. Your design or the gardener's?"

"David, I am the gardener," she states, smiling like a proud kid with an A on her report card. "I planted the plants in the pattern you see. I don't mind getting my hands dirty."

Looking at her square on, my guess is that she is 15 to 17 years younger than me. Her youth causes me to think of

Daphne and why I'm here. The near-perfect garden doesn't go along with the shameful information in the folder I hold. I wish we had stayed in the library. I sit next to her on the circular bench inside the gazebo.

"David, from your call I was expecting you earlier. What happened?"

"I went to see your ex-husband. He was involved in something that warranted an immediate response."

"Oh, and did you deal with the matter?"

"Not completely." She hasn't mentioned my thug-like behaviors last night, so I won't bring it up either. And I certainly don't see the importance of telling her that my delay in meeting her was due to me making her ex piss his pants.

"Well, as I'm sure you are aware by now, he is not a man to deal with in a hesitant manner. You must deal with him quickly. He is never idle, be warned."

The need to tell her how criminal her ex-husband's involvement is, is not urgent. I don't want her to view my attack on him as personal. He has affected our community as a whole, and has hurt her personally.

"If you don't mind me asking, Eleanor, how did you meet your ex-husband?" Most of the story I have been told by Daphne, but I need to get her talking about him and hopefully stirring up some hate for the man.

"Daphne, bless her soul . . ." She stops. She doesn't cry, but she does have to catch her breath. She's looking at me, but also through me. Eleanor is in thought.

"Daphne sent Randolph's business to me. I did his data entry for about six months. You see, I ran my own legal data-entry service. Later, I moved into doing a few referrals for the firm.

"I received my paralegal certificate eighteen months after high school. The program I completed directed its students toward entrepreneurship. At no time did I think of working for a firm. I went after contracts from law firms, not employment."

Daphne said Eleanor was one of Peal's best bird-dogs before they were married. Why would Eleanor say "a few" referrals?

"You said you did referrals as well?"

"Yes, that turned out to be the largest percentage of my billing. I didn't expect it. It started out as a sideline. Randolph asked me to keep an eye out for people injured or sick or involved in any type of accident."

"And your company did the data entry on your referrals?"

"Yes, we did most of them, why?"

"I was curious as to how much you knew about the auto accident cases."

"I was well-informed, David."

"Oh." I give her my serious, narrow-eyed, no-smile, firm look.

She smiles, not intimidated in the slightest, "If you are asking if I knew about Randolph's involvement prior to the courtroom, my answer to you in this garden is yes; outside of this garden my answer is no." The smile changes to the confident, assured look of a polished professional.

It's apparent to me that it is time to play hardball. As she says, Peal was never idle and I need to make things happen fast. I don't have time for niceties.

"And you lost your mother in an auto accident didn't you?"

"Yes, I did." Curiosity as to where the question is going fills her eyes. I don't want to hurt her, but she has to have this information.

"A car rear-ended by a truck struck her church bus. All the bus and car passengers were killed instantly. Randolph

Peal and Associates represented the church and the family in the car. The suit put the trucking company out of business. It was one of the largest settlements of an auto accident in this city. It pretty much put Randolph and his firm on the map."

"Yes, they broke through with that case." She is beginning to fidget with the wicker of the gazebo bench and her eyes are watering. I have to push because Peal has to go down.

"And you and Randolph were married soon after."

"Yes, he became very important to me after my mother's death. My mother motivated me. Are your parents still alive, David?"

I note her attempt to change the subject and smile. Truly gardening is not this 'round-the-way girl's only talent. "Yes, both my parents are still alive."

"Consider yourself blessed. I miss my mother every day. My going into the paralegal program was all her idea. She secured the loans that bought the computers and data-entry software I needed to start the business. She was an office clerk most of her life. She would tell me 'it was honest work, but work for someone else is just that; for someone else.'

"Her goal for me was to get my own. She pushed me to succeed. When she died, I lost interest in my business and life in general.

"But Randolph kept sending me work, so I kept doing it. Eventually we started dating and one thing led to another. It wasn't a hot love affair. I don't know if I ever loved him. There was a void in my life and he filled it. Eventually his firm bought my business and we married. I was his wife until one day I realized that was all I'd become: his wife. My mother raised me to be more.

"He didn't want me to return to work, but saw nothing

wrong with me taking classes. I guess he thought I was taking all gardening classes or something. He was shocked into a stupor when I told him I was a year away from sitting for my law exams. I didn't hide my coursework from him. He never asked what I was studying. And as long as I went to the community affairs on his arm he was fine."

"African-American community affairs," I say.

She's looking at me as if she is trying find something in my face. She sighs. "Mr. Price, do you know who Randolph's father is?"

"No."

"Well, you should find out before you pass judgment on me or him. It's a little more complicated than you think." I think that if she were five years younger, she would have rolled her eyes at me, but maturity caused her to only pause.

"After my mother's death, nothing much mattered: who I married, if I worked, nothing. However, once I got back to myself, back to wanting life, Randolph and I began having problems.

"He didn't want me to get a law degree. He went as far as removing his law books from the library. Can you believe that? I got the degree though, and Randolph is out of my life. I open my own law office in six more days. My time with Randolph wasn't wasted. I learned and earned from that time."

"So you knew he built up his firm on staged auto accidents?"

"Yes." I hear the annoyance in her tone. "I referred people to him. People who wanted to earn fast money and were not afraid to take a chance. They all knew what they were doing."

"Did you know that . . . your mother . . . your mother's death was the result of one of his accidents going bad?"

"Say again."

"The car that crashed into your mother's church bus was driven by one of his drivers."

"You are mistaken. It may have been a staged accident, but Randolph's people didn't stage it. I would have known about it."

"Not if he chose to keep it from you; which was what he did."

"No. If what you are saying is true . . . then, I too . . . was involved in my mother's death."

"No, not you, him. He was and is guilty. He kept his dirty deed from you."

"David, you have been misguided."

"No. I am not the misguided one here. Daphne Nelson swore to it, and I believe she went to her death because of it. She said you would recognize the driver's name. Inside this folder is information that supports what I have told you." I'm passing the folder to her. She's looking at the folder as if it is papers from Satan. It's a hard statement, but I have to say it. "Randolph Peal killed your mother."

"No! No! You are mistaken, that was an accident! My mother's death was an accident! A real accident! Mr. Price, you have to leave. Right now! Get out! Get off of my land!"

She stands abruptly and is running from me and the folder; trampling through the beautiful garden. I leave the folder on the bench. That was the most distasteful thing I've done in recent memory.

# Chapter Thirteen

I don't like feeling regretful about my actions; second-guessing myself after the fact is useless. What was done is done. I'll call Eleanor back this evening. Perhaps she'll listen.

Part of the original plan Ricky, Regina and I came up with was to meet over Regina's after giving Eleanor the information. But since I aborted the plan by going to Peal's office first, I doubt they would be over Regina's. Why I'm driving up her block now is uncertain, but I must not be too far off base because Ricky's truck is parked in front of Regina's house.

The "House Sold" sign stands in the front yard. At first I wasn't agitated by her selling the house; however, actually seeing the sign pisses me off and I don't know why. I purposely kick it over walking through her lawn to the front porch.

"Sold my damn house, selfish heifer," I mumble under my breath as I knock on her door. The door opens with my first rap. Walking in, I yell, "Hey, who's here?"

"Back here, D." Ricky is whispering.

In the kitchen, Ricky and Gina's backs are to me. They're looking at Attorney Peal, who is wearing my sunglasses. His face appears stuck to the window of the back door. He's outside looking in. He's not moving at all. Looking closer, I see blood around his mouth, and through the blue lenses of my sunglasses I notice his eyes are popped open, but motionless. He looks dead.

Dead in my damn Gucci sunglasses!

"Oh shit. Did you call the police?" Neither Gina nor Ricky answers me. Gina has the cordless in her hand, trembling. Ricky's arm is wrapped around her shoulder.

"Give me the phone, Gina. You called, that's all you can do, darlin'. Now let the phone go."

She releases the phone to Ricky and turns to me and asks, "Why did you do it here, David? I told you I was going to stop the adoption! Do you hate me that much? Why did you do it, David? And why did you do it here?"

She draws back and slaps me hard, real damn hard.

"You murdering bastard!"

"What the . . ." is my response.

Pushing between us, Ricky says, "D, you better get out of here, partner. Man she called da police and was screaming you did it in da phone. She was panickin', man. We saw the back of ya car burnin' rubber out of da alley when we pulled up."

"What?"

"You can explain later, but now, bro, you gots to go! Hit me on the cell in 'bout an hour. Get on now!"

Running from the house, I have no idea where I'm going. Driving down the block, I decide running is not such a good idea. I pull into the alley behind Gina's house, open her garage and park inside. I pull down her overhead door and stand the shadows of the garage.

"Damn, she's tripping! Why the fuck she tell the police I killed him? How could she believe that?"

I leave the garage in stealth mode. From the foot of the back stairs I see that a push broom has fallen behind the shyster's back and is keeping him propped against the window. His death doesn't stop the anger I feel toward him. I still hate his ass. I sneak down to the basement door and hope Regina hasn't changed the locks. She hasn't.

Creeping up the stairs to the kitchen door, I stop and listen. She and Ricky are talking.

"You know he didn't do this, Gina."

"We saw his car, Ricky."

"He ain't the only man that drives a black Caddy, Gina."

"His is the only black Caddy that has reason to be speeding out of this alley."

"You don't know that."

"Tell it to the police Ricky. His heart is full of hate for Randolph."

"You know what D is and is not capable of, Gina."

"No I don't! Him being involved with Daphne proves that. I have no idea what that man is capable of. Did you see the rage he was in this morning, merely because I called Randolph? He smashed my phone into the ground. I have never seen him in that state. He is not the man I married. He did it, Ricky; as sure as you and I are standing here. He shot Randolph."

The Harvey police are coming in the front and back doors. Heavy steps above me have dust falling from the rafters of the basement. They order Ricky to the floor. Regina starts screaming. A female voice tells her to calm down. I hear a slap.

"Bitch! I'll have your job if you put your hands on me again." That's Regina.

Walking to the rear basement window, I hear shuffling

on the back porch. Peeping out, I see the paramedics laying the shyster on a stretcher. This is the first time I can remember smiling at a corpse. I feel light in the shoulders and loose at the knees. If I weren't hiding I'd sing out loud in joy.

Awgh man, cops are coming out of the garage! More cops are bringing Regina down the back stairs. She's denying knowing anything about the car being in the garage. I turn around because I hear cops coming down the basement steps. Regina's at the outside door with more cops. There is no place to hide. Cops are in front of and behind me. I put my hands up. I'm being pushed to the floor anyway. Cuffed and disarmed, they are taking me up to the kitchen.

They seat me in a kitchen chair next to a handcuffed Ricky. We see each other and start laughing. This has happened with us since childhood; when one sees the other in a tight position we laugh. It works as stress relief for whoever is in the tight spot. Laughing now does make me feel a little better.

Laughing, however, causes me to catch a cop's elbow in the back of my head. He's apologizing through a grin. Regina's not laughing; matter of fact, she's not even smiling. She's looking at me as if I nailed Jesus to the cross. She turns away, crying. The passage "Oh ye of little faith" enters my mind.

Ricky, who is dressed in his walking suit, says in a real low tone, "Don't sweat it, D. She'll be awight. A lot of stuff in her head right now that's all."

"Shut up!" bellows the elbowing cop to Ricky. I hope he doesn't elbow Ricky in the head, because that would escalate the whole situation. Ricky hits back, he always has.

A lady officer escorts Regina out of the kitchen to the

front room. There are eight cops in the kitchen with Ricky and me. I can hear Regina telling someone about seeing my car speeding out the alley.

"She's trying her best to cook you, boss. She must be really upset 'bout that white boy dyin', huh? And you being with Daphne ain't help a bit. Think about it, bro. You now killed her rich white man and screwed her younger friend. Yeah, she wants ya ass under da jailhouse."

Ricky thinks what he just said is real funny. He wants to burst out in laughter. I can tell because his eyes are starting to water and his whole face is straining from muffling the laugh.

This situation ain't funny, but if I don't turn away from him I will laugh; turning in my chair I say, "I didn't kill anyone, Ricky."

He bites down on his lip and takes a deep breath, regaining some composure, and says, "You know what I'm sayin', bro. She think ya killed him. I know you wouldn't kill nobody." He tries to scoot his big self closer to me unnoticed. How he thinks these police ain't going to notice almost 400 pounds of yellow mass inching over in a chair, I don't know. The chair sounds off with a loud scrape moving across the floor.

He ignores the obvious noise and whispers, "Where was you at, anyway?"

"I went out to Eleanor's."

"Good, 'cause you gonna need an alibi with Gina helpin' ya like she is." This time he doesn't even try to hold his laughter. I would laugh with him if not for the fact that Detectives Dixon and Lee from the Chicago Police Department walk into the kitchen.

"Look, Lee, it's the security guard and his fat boy. They stay around murder scenes, don't they?"

Dixon's breath is always foul. His skin is bad and his clothes are cheap. He is standing behind me talking to his red, reggae-singer-looking partner Lee. I don't trust neither one of them. I have never heard about them doing a person wrong. My distrust comes from me being a black man and them being cops.

"Uncuff the fat one and get him out of here. It looks like the security guard is the winner today."

Two of the uniformed officers take Ricky to the front. Lee sits across from me, and Dixon remains standing behind me. I have been in this position before.

"The lady up front is convinced you capped ole' boy on the back porch." Lee picked up the gun the officers disarmed me of in the basement and sniffs it. "Well, you didn't shoot him with this one did you?"

"I didn't shoot him at all. But tell me, detective, why are two Chicago Police detectives in my face? This is Harvey, Illinois; isn't this out of your jurisdiction?"

"Don't worry about it, boy. We can arrest *your* black ass in Denver if we want to."

The officers snicker. This isn't right and I know it. "I want to call a lawyer."

"You can call your mama for all I care. You see, I got a restraining order filed by the corpse against you. I got the same man dead on your ex-wife's back porch. I got your ex-wife swearing she saw you burning rubber out of the alley not twenty minutes ago. I got an office filled with lawyers who say you put a pistol to his head this morning, and threatened his life. All that got me a warrant for your arrest, which means your ass is mine in Harvey, Kentucky or New York. Buddy, unless you got a damn good alibi for your time since you left the victim's office this morning, you better get used to county wear."

He stands and Dixon pulls me up from the back. "Let's

go, Mr. Personal Security Guard. I got some persons that need securing down in lockup."

It is the cops' turn to laugh, and they laugh it up good.

Cuffed in the back of an unmarked police car is not a place I like to be seen. The neighbors who don't work nine to five on Regina's block are out in full force. Four black detectives are arguing outside the unmarked car I'm in. It appears Dixon and Lee can't take me. I'm being held as a murder suspect for a crime that occurred in Harvey. The Harvey cops want to lock me up in Markham.

Looking around at all the police cars, it occurs to me that I don't see the shyster Peal's car. His BMW SUV wasn't anywhere on the street and I didn't see it parked in the back. How the hell had he gotten to Regina's?

The two Harvey detectives quickly jump into the front seat of the unmarked car I'm in and pull off, leaving Dixon and Lee smelling their exhaust.

"Who the hell do they think they are? They think they can roll up on our collar and ride with it? Not today. We got an unsolved-murder rate too. This sucker is getting locked down and tried in our court. We're getting credit for this slam dunk."

They are talking about me as if I'm not even here. And a brother like me remains silent. They radio in my arrival. Dispatch tells them not to bring me to Markham lockup. I am to be transported to the Morgan Park police station in Chicago.

The officer driving brakes the car hard, slamming me into the bulletproof divider. They think that's funny. Laughing, the driver U-turns and we're heading to the city. They're laughing, but I can tell the both of them are as mad as a poor fat man with no food stamps. And a pissed-off cop ain't nobody's friend.

At least with Dixon and Lee I kind of know what to expect. These two suckers got a brother nervous, sitting up there cursing, slamming their fists on the dashboard and elbowing windows. The driver pulls off the avenue into an alley and parks behind a grocery/liquor store. The alley is open at both ends, and people are walking by.

It's not the perfect place to beat a cuffed man, but it will do. The two detectives get out. The cop on the passenger side opens my door. It's left open as they walk around to the front of the store. Cuffed, I remain in the seat. Leaving is not an option for an intelligent man.

On their return to the alley, one of them says, "Stupid is still in the car. I guess he wants to go to prison." My door is slammed hard. "Coward ass motherfucker," one of them says.

He's right. I am a coward, coward enough not to run down an alley in handcuffs. The ride to the station remains rough as they continue to make sharp turns and hit every pothole and rise in the road. Sweet Jesus, I never thought seeing a jailhouse would cause me to feel relieved, but seeing the Morgan Park station takes the tightness out of my chest.

This is not my first time at this lockup. When Ricky and I were teenagers, we took my brother Charlie's '65 Chevy Impala and went racing down 111th street. We were racing against a yellow Ford Maverick. It must have been a V8 because it was giving us a hell of a run.

Ricky had the Impala floored, and all four barrels of the carburetor were wide open. My brother's glass-packed pipes were roaring. We were pulling away from the Maverick when the cops appeared out of nowhere, gaining with lights flashing. We couldn't go any faster if we wanted to. The Impala was giving us all she had.

What sealed our fate was the Impala running out of gas. It coughed to a stop and the squad was on us, but they sped past, chasing the Maverick. If we'd some gas we might have gotten away, but another squad pulled up and we were off to jail.

The Morgan Park station hasn't changed much. It is just as dingy and musty as it was back then. The Harvey city detectives sit me on a hard plastic bench in front of the desk. They are saying something I can't hear. The cop at the desk hands them another pair of cuffs. The driver takes his cuffs off me and replaces them with the ones the cop at the desk gave him. The Harvey cops are gone without a goodbye.

The place seems pretty busy for the middle of the day, but then again, maybe it's not. I'm not here often enough to know if this is busy. People are continuously walking by, but I am the only one in cuffs. I ask repeatedly for a phone call. No response. I ask why I am being held. No response. To my left is the door leading to the holding cells. It opens, and out walk Dixon and Lee.

"Glad you could make it," Lee says, patting me on my head as they walk by.

A chubby cop in a white shirt greets them in front of the desk. Neither of the three look in my direction as they talk about me. Dixon requests an interrogation room. They are talking in hushed, hurried tones, anxious to question me. The white shirt has a room cleared for them, so Lee uncuffs me from the bench and yanks me up by my belt, causing the belt buckle to dig into my stomach. One day I'm going to get with his dreadlock-wearing ass in the worst way, one day soon.

He spins me around and slams me into the wall behind the plastic bench. The cuffs are back on, and I am being pushed through the door leading to the holding cells. All the cells are empty. The one in the center has open bars. Lee shoves me in and slams the bars behind me.

Stumbling to keep my balance, I keep my mouth shut. What I want to say will get me locked up for sure. To my back I hear, "all right Mr. Security Escort, where you been all morning and afternoon?

"Now, this is what I want you tell me; I want to hear that you hung out in the garage and waited for the lawyer. Okay? Then I want you to tell me when Attorney Peal came down to the garage you kidnapped him and whipped his ass. You understand what I want to hear?"

Turning around to face them I say, "I hadn't seen Attorney Peal until I got to Regina's house."

Quickly walking up to the bars, Lee yells, "Stop lying! You were in his office this morning!"

"Yeah, I was with him this morning, but not this afternoon." For a brief second panic tries to set in, then I remember my alibi: Eleanor. Hopefully I was with her at the time Peal was shot. No need in offering this information now. Listening to what they have is best.

"Bullshit. You saw him this afternoon and shot him in the head, but what I don't understand is why you took him to your ex-wife's house. What was that all about?"

"I didn't shoot that man."

"Yes, you did."

"No, I didn't."

Calmer, Lee says, "You did it, but I'm certain it was an accident, wasn't it? Admit it now and it will go better for you later."

It's time for me to act irate. I yell, "Man, ain't no sign on my head that say Booboo the Fool! I want my phone call now. Not now; but right now! I know my damn rights!"

Dixon and Lee are not in their precinct—the chance of them beating me outside of their domain is slight, so I'm barking a bit.

"The only rights you got is the right to the ass kicking Dixon is about to give you! Can we interrogate this witness alone?" Lee asks the cop in the white shirt.

"Not a problem." Leaving, the white shirt says to me, "See you later, tough guy."

I'm not scared, but I am backing away from the bars as Lee unlocks them. Dixon enters, smiling.

"My lawyer will sue you until I'm spending your great-grandkids' money if you put a hand on me."

"I'm sterile, douche bag. Won't be having no great-grandkids."

I'm lowering my knees, attempting to get a good center of gravity, I can't punch, but I can kick. I ain't just taking a beating. He is going to have to bring some to get some.

Seeing me get into position he asks, "What, you gonna fight me back? Oh, I like that."

I'm on my toes, shuffling a little, hoping to find a good solid stance that will allow front snap kicks.

"Look at him, Lee. He's ready to go at it. Dancing on his toes. You think he knows something? Got me kinda scared. Stop your prancing before you give yourself a heart attack, Mr. Security Escort. I'm coming to take off the cuffs. Your partner and fat buddy are here to pick you up."

I don't stop moving.

"If you kick me, I'll shoot you. I swear to God I will." He draws his revolver. "Now turn around and face the wall."

Trusting this cop is not on my to-do list, especially with the sneaky smile on Lee's face.

"Man I'm not turning my back to you. Have my partner come in here; then I'll turn around."

It's Dixon who takes a couple steps back, "Detective Lee, you have sparked distrust in this man's heart. Go get his partner."

Lee leaves the holding area. Dixon, shaking his head in disbelief, says, "After all we been through, you don't trust me."

"All we been through? Our relationship consists of you and the red Bob Marley arresting me. How is that going through something?"

"'The Red Bob Marley.' That's a good one. I might use that one on him myself." Putting his pistol back in his holster, he says, "We've done a little more than arrest you, Price. A couple of months ago we did visit you at the hospital."

"Visit? Man, y'all interrogated me on my deathbed. That wasn't a visit."

Saying that brings a smile to both our faces. I turn my back to him and he releases the handcuffs.

"We don't think you did this one, Price, but everything is pointing in your direction. Help us and yourself. Stay out of it until we get a handle on what's going on. I am going to say this again: Keep away from this case. It's in your best interest to not be involved."

Turning around, I face him. I'm expecting him to extend his hand to shake. He doesn't. I follow him out to the front of the station. Amid the crowd at the front desk I spot Ricky and Carol. She looks relieved to see me. Ricky is laughing at me.

At the desk, Carol hands me a plastic bag full of the belongings the police stripped me of.

"After Ricky called this morning and told me about you going to Randolph's office, I took the liberty of contacting Eleanor myself. She told me you met with her. That was probably the smartest thing you've done all day."

The insult is accompanied with a slight smile, very slight. The three of us walk from the desk to the plastic bench against the wall.

"I think whatever you said to her along with the news of Daphne and Stanley's deaths sparked her to want to meet with us."

Ricky let out a loud grunt and says, "Man, who cares? I mean da lawyer is dead, there is no threat of him adopting Chester. It's time to go home, man. Don't get all caught up in dis. Let dem cops do they job."

"Daphne and Stanley were killed on my porch, Ricky. I got to find out what I can."

"What's to find out? We know da lawyer killed dem!"

"Yeah, but who killed the lawyer!"

"Why you care who killed him? Just get ya own alibi straight—fuck dat white boy!"

Clipping the cell phone on my belt, I ask Carol, "Did they leave my car at Regina's?" I place my foot up on the bench and begin inserting my gym-shoe laces.

"No, the cop with the dreadlocks had it towed downtown. These police are serious, David. I disagree with Ricky. You need to keep working on this case. You are their prime suspect."

"No, not any more. Detective Dixon assured me of that." I toss the plastic bag in a tall silver trash receptacle and walk towards the door.

Carol's not following me to the door. I stop. "What?" I ask her.

"If you're not a suspect, then perhaps you can explain why they impounded your car and got a search warrant for your home and office."

She has a point. I tell her and Ricky, "Dixon gave the impression that I was off the hook."

"Mmh, well his actions show otherwise." She folds her

arms across her small chest. Across the busy room I spot Dixon and Lee. Dixon nods his head and waves goodbye. Lee flips me the bird.

"Bastards. Let's get out of here."

Outside in the parking lot, dark clouds have moved across the sky. Thunder sounds and a light drizzle starts. Yet none of us hurry to Ricky's Expedition. He asks me, "Do you remember when we ran out of gas in your brother's Chevy and ended up here?"

"Yeah man, I remember."

"That was your fault too."

"How you figure? . . . Never mind, dude."

The cool, misty rain feels too good to run from; we stroll across the lot. I should call Daphne's parents; I imagine they have questions they want answered. "Carol, could you find a phone number for Daphne's parents out in Harvey? I need to call them."

"No problem, boss. Are you coming to the office?"

"No. Ricky and I are going to see a man about a dog. Call me with the number."

Carol stopped walking, gave me a hug and a strange look, "You watch yourself, Mr. Price. Somebody involved in this is not afraid to kill. I don't want you to be next." She walks over to her car which was parked across from Ricky's truck.

He yells to her, "Hey, what about me? Ain't ya gonna tell me to be careful?"

She doesn't answer, only waves and gets into her jazzy little Benz.

"She knows she wants me. She needs to stop playin' hard to get."

"She don't want you, man, and you the one who needs to stop. I thought you were putting an end to all that flirting and carrying on anyway."

"Who told ya dat?"

"You did, and your actions. You're not hanging out, you staying around the house and your speeches about the streets not having nothing for you. I just figured you had settled down."

"All dat is true, my brother. I am finished with street life and my clubbin' and gamblin' days are limited, but partner let's not get beside ourselves. Chasin' tail is inbred. I cain't do a thang about dat. Yeah, I slowed down on it, but if I see a slimmie dat's gonna let me, I'm on it."

"Well that slimmie is not going to let you."

"Yeah dat's what you say, but I got her comin' around. She be trying' to hold back the smiles. I make her laugh, but she just don't want to show it."

Opening the door-locks with his alarm clicker, he asks, "Look-a-here man, where we goin'?"

"I need to get with that lawyer Martin. We're headed downtown to the law offices. Then, if you don't mind, out to Daphne's folks'." The rain is getting a little heavier.

"Okay, I'm wit'cha, bro. A brotha was gettin' bored anyway. I might as well stop somebody from puttin' a slug in my ace." Inside the truck he pulls a Howlin' Wolf CD from the compartment holder. "Slide dat in tha changer, wouldcha?"

Howlin' Wolf's rusty voice fills the truck as we head to the loop.

"*Three hundred pounds of heavenly joy,*" Ricky is sharing the lead with Wolf; he sounds a lot like him. We are parked on LaSalle Street in front of the high-rise that houses Peal's office.

"So why are you goin' to see dis lawyer?" he asks over the music.

"He is one of the few people left to question. All I got is him and Eleanor; one of them has to know something." I cut the music off to stop from screaming. Ricky plays the blues as loud as kids play rap.

"I understand talkin' to Eleanor, Peal was involved with her mother dyin'. But what's da deal with dis Martin guy, how did Peal hurt him?"

"I don't know. Right now I'm hoping Martin will be a point of reference. I've got to gather information. I'm close to working blind on this."

"You want me to go up with you, in case he tries to throw you out?"

"No, I can handle it."

As soon as I walk into the law office, the receptionist jumps from the desk and backs up against the wall as if I was pointing a gun at her. I actually see her legs trembling under her gray pleated skirt.

"What, what, what . . . what is it that you want!" She is on the brink of hysterics. She grabs the phone, "I'm calling the police!"

I turn around to see if it is me who has her wigging out, and it is; she and I are the only occupants of the reception area. "Miss, I'm here to see Martin."

"Attorney MacNard is not here!"

"What did you say?"

"I said Attorney MacNard is not here! I'm calling the police!"

Hearing Martin's last name stops me in my tracks. MacNard. That was the family name from the trucking company. I turn around to leave and push the call button for the elevator. The door opens immediately: Martin is on the elevator dressed in a dark brown suit that swallows him up. A tiny dark brother in a dark suit, he barely has a presence. We pass each other, staring. He keeps those pigeon-egg eyes on me as we pass each other. He doesn't say a thing, and neither do I. The doors close and I ride down. The library is my destination.

Snatching Ricky's truck door open, I jump in and demand, "Get me to a library, man. Didn't you say that the man who ran Aspire trucking, which was the trucking company involved in the church bus accident, was named MacNard?"

"Yeah." Starting the truck, he pulls directly into traffic.

"Martin—the lawyer upstairs—his last name is MacNard."

"No shit, the lawyer's last name is MacNard? Did you ask him about it?"

"No, I want to check it out first. It can't be that many black MacNards in one city."

"You right 'bout dat."

Ricky pulls up to the Harold Washington Library on the Van Buren Street side. He cuts on his flashers and gets out with me. I'm surprised, but I don't object, being that I understand how it is when one is on the trail of a clue. The case is picking up and Ricky wants to be on point with the discoveries.

He insists on finding the information online. Personally, I want to go to the microfilm room, but Ricky's idea proves better. Sitting at one of many terminals in the reference section of the library, Ricky not only finds the information, but he finds it in less than five minutes. The death notice of Matthew MacNard provides us with needed information: he was survived by his wife, Mildred, and two sons, Martin and Michael.

"Good job, bro. I would still be looking through film."

"You better get with this here digital age; all kind of info is online, partner. Now look-a-here, if I'm understandin' this right, it looks like Martin is Matthew MacNard's son.

And we know that Matthew MacNard ran Aspire Trucking."

"Right."

"But this means Martin is working for the people that sued his daddy."

"It looks that way."

"Somethin' is goin' on here, D." We both stand from the terminal. Ricky doesn't close the screen as we both walk away. A kid hops right on the terminal and Matthew MacNard's death notice is gone. Looking around I notice the reference section is now flooded with young students with backpacks. We must have only been steps ahead of them because now there is not one available terminal.

Riding the escalator down, Ricky turns his head to me and asks "Are you thinkin' about this man? Two people who had they lives ruined by the church bus accident are right next to Peal: his wife and one of his partners in business. Now that's a strong coincidence."

I hear Ricky, but while exiting the library I can't help but think about the great man it was named after, Chicago's first African-American Mayor, Harold Washington.

April 12, 1983 was a day of celebration for African-American Chicago. Well, most of Chicago partied, but us blacks really partied. We danced in the streets, at our jobs, in churches and all around and through City Hall. We finally had representation. We were finally a recognized force within the city. We, the collective force of black citizens called "The Sleeping Giant," had made our presence known and picked who we wanted to run the city. Damn, that felt good!

I was swollen with pride that day. You could not have paid me to stop grinning. It was a black man running the city. Not a puppet or a figurehead, but our elected official. For the first time in my life I more than just lived in

Chicago; for once I was part of it. I watched city council meetings on TV, read all the political articles in the newspapers and even got involved in my ward. I was a concerned citizen. Then they killed him.

A brother like me is one of those Chicagoans who will go to our grave believing that Harold Washington was murdered. The man meant too much for me to just accept his death. And being mayor meant too much to him to die. In my heart, I will always feel as though he was murdered.

Standing on Van Buren under the El tracks, Ricky hacks a glob of mucus into the street, "You know what, D? In my opinion both of them, Eleanor and Martin, shoulda killed his ass. You got some real suspects now."

He opens the locks with his alarm pad and we climb into the truck, "Maybe they hooked dis up together? You need to find out if they know each other. I hope they ain't hooked up fo' yo sake. Ain't no tellin' what type of payback shit they could be comin' up with. I'm tellin' you, bro, you better leave this here case alone. These folks is lookin' for retribution."

I seriously doubt that Eleanor and Martin are cohorts, but it is time to talk to Martin. This time I want Ricky to go upstairs with me; there is safety in numbers.

"Ricky, I need to go back to the law office."

"Naw, man, you need to rest. You been through enough in one day. I know I have. We will pick up da trail in da morning; just goin' and goin' ain't gonna undo what happened. It's time to rest, bro. I'm taking you home. Besides, my kids is finished with all they programs and stuff and Martha is home alone with them, and she is too strict on them by herself. I got to get home to keep the peace."

I offer no protest. He is right; merely hearing the word "rest" makes me tired. But I don't want to stop. If I keep going I won't have to think about Daphne or Stanley. I lean back in the seat and listen to Howlin' Wolf the entire trip home.

When I wake, Ricky is in front of my house, parked behind a cleaning van. The lady from the cleaning service is walking down my porch stairs; this isn't her day to clean. I get out of the truck and go to her.

"Hello, Mr. Price."

"Madelyn, how are you?"

The blood that had run down the steps is gone.

"I am well, sir. I hope you don't mind, but we cleaned your steps. We were scheduled for the Harrises across the street, and once we finished ,we did your steps. There will be no extra charge, sir. And we are sorry for your loss. And, Mr. Price, I want to thank for the business you have sent our way; you were our first customer in Englewood. Because you trusted us, a lot of others folks use our service now. Thanks, sir."

She turns and gets into her van. When she pulls off, so does Ricky. I am left alone, so I go into the house.

This is the emptiest the house has felt in a while. If not for Yin and Yang's warm, stubby-tail-wagging greetings; I would have gone out to a bar and got drunk but I have my dogs. I go into the back yard with them. If it wasn't getting dark I would go work in my garden.

Sitting on the steps, I watch them pee on different parts of the fence and trees that line my yard. They both find spots to squat for a dump. It's like they are rushing to see who will finish their business first. The phone is ringing in the kitchen, so I rise to go answer it.

It's a social worker calling on my bother Robert's behalf. He is about to finish a twenty-one-day treatment program, and she wants to know if my home is a stable, drug-free environment for him. I tell her yes. She asks if there's a problem with him residing in the home. I tell her no, there is no problem, he is welcome here. She tells me he will be released in two days, and they will provide transportation to my address. She thanks me and hangs up.

We, the family, were all worried about my bother Robert; my parents more than my brother Charles or me. No one had heard from him in over two months. Charles and I figured he was with a woman who got high like him—that has been his MO for a couple of years. We don't hear from him when he has hooked into a woman who will buy his drugs. But, I did feel something was different about him being gone this time. I knew he was getting tired of the crackhead lifestyle and I hoped he was in treatment.

I call my parents to share the good news with them; my father answers. He's happy about the news because he sent twenty dollars to the center two weeks ago for Robert to get cigarettes and candy and my mother sent him new gym shoes, khaki pants and underwear. He wasn't sure twenty-one days was enough time, but he says it's a good start, and I agree.

He tells me my mother has gone to play bingo and poker at the Catholic church around the corner, and all she cooked for him were some boiled potatoes and Polish sausages: "It is a damn shame she waited until she turned seventy-two to start gambling and hanging with white folks. Silly woman didn't even leave no bread for the sausages. Well I got to get on to the market. I'ma tell her you called, David. Love you, boy."

I tell him I love him too, and that ends our conversation.

I let the dogs in, and the three of us stretch out in the living room. I decide not to go upstairs to my bedroom; it's not that I don't want to think about Daphne, I just don't want to be sad. I flip the channels until I find *Sanford and Son* and settle on the couch for the night.

I awake to the dogs barking at the front doorbell. I know it's Ricky; they only bark at him. I open the door and he hands me a cup of coffee and says he'll be waiting in the truck. Yeah, the mystery bug has beaten him good. I drink the coffee in the shower because I am anxious to get back on the trail as well. I slide into a pair of Levi's and a white Polo golf shirt, one big enough to hang over my pistols. I slip into my Cole Haan sandals and head out to the truck.

"To the lawyer's, right?" is the greeting Ricky gives me. He is dressed in a yellow walking suit, with beige bone-colored gator sandals. Most people wouldn't wear a short suit downtown, but my best friend isn't most people.

"You got it, boss. To the Loop."

Howlin' Wolf is still playing in the changer, and I am glad to hear him, and to be with my boy.

We aren't off the elevator a good second before the receptionist, Ms. Panic Panties, is dialing the phone, "He's back, sir! And he has someone with him . . . conference room A, right away, sir."

Keeping what she considers a safe distance, the receptionist stands and says, "This way."

She takes us to the same conference room Daphne and I were in before. Ricky and I sit at the card tables. "Tacky," Ricky says loud enough for the fleeing receptionist to hear.

She, Martin and an older white man almost collide outside the door. When I look at the older guy there is something slightly familiar about him that I can't place. He is wearing a well-tailored suit cut wide in the thigh, much like the ones I wear, and the hand-sewn shirt he's wearing has the same style monogrammed letters on his French cuffs mine have. As he walks past me in the conference room I catch a whiff of sandalwood body oil. I didn't know white people wore body oils.

The Rolex on his wrist is the platinum version of my gold one. What's familiar is that this guy dresses like me. Ricky leans to my ear and whispers, "The motherfucker is wearin' gators."

I look down and sure enough, he is in a pair of black, square-toe gators. Ricky and I give each other the nod. No matter what comes out this white-looking man's face, we agree that he is black.

"Good day, gentlemen, I am Peter Peal, and I'm certain you've met Martin." He's waiting for our introduction.

"I'm David Price, and this is my associate, Richard Brown."

"Ah! I know both you gentlemen by reputation. Mr. Brown, you have turned around quite a few failing liquor stores on the south side, and I applaud your hiring of our young men. I served on a combined church board with your wife last summer. We helped with the planning of the Gospel Festival. It is so good to meet you, sir." Peter Peal extends his hand and Ricky stands to shake it.

"Wait a minute," Ricky tilts his globe recalling, "is your firm the one that does the taxes and estate planning?"

I have to take a second look at Ricky because he is actually pronouncing the *th* sound. This hasn't occurred around my ears since we were at the university together. The only time I heard him attempt to modify his pronunciation was when he was speaking to a professor. Very seldom does my friend say, "the," "this," "that," or "them," he is more comfortable with, "da," "dis," "dat" and "dem." But like most black people, Ricky can turn off his Ebonics when needed.

"Yes," Peter Peal answers.

"Yeah, I'm familiar, Zondervan and Peal. This guy was

your son?" Ricky's emphasis causes Peal to cut his eyes to me; he's trying to understand Ricky's tone. My expression tells him nothing. If he doesn't know his son was a shyster I won't be the one to tell him.

"Yes. Randolph was actually my oldest son. His mother and I were together in college. I have three other sons from my marriage. They have all joined me in the tax firm you're familiar with, Mr. Brown."

Ricky returns to his folding chair and the senior Peal turns his attention to me. Along with his hue, he and his son share the same dishwater-blond hair, except his is speckled with gray strands. I suspect the senior Peal is in his early sixties.

"And Mr. Price, the only minority-owned bodyguard service in the state, not to mention the beautiful rehabilitation you have been doing in Englewood. Your work has brought other investors back to the area." We shake hands as Martin stands there looking totally uninformed. I guess he thought a brother like me was broke.

"Gentlemen, I do believe we will be more comfortable in my son's office. Martin, will you kindly see to the coffee and sandwiches? Thank you. Mr. Brown and Mr. Price, please follow me."

I'm flattered that he is conscious of who I am, but he has also put me on guard. This is a silky-smooth man. Realizing that within the type of law he practices a degree of marketing is required, common sense tells me I shouldn't be threatened by his acquaintance with me. If one is doing estate planning, one must be informed on who has money. Nonetheless, him being better informed of me than I am of him has my senses on alert.

We have to walk past the receptionist and she shares the same flabbergasted expression as Martin. When we enter the private office, the older Peal sits behind the desk, and Ricky and I take the leather couch.

"And how may I be of service to you gentleman?"

It is a simple question and he seems sincere in asking it, but the peace-making tone of his voice left me uneasy. Even though he is asking to be of service, I'm feeling like the target.

"Well actually, Mr. Peal, we came to speak with Martin. I am looking into the death of Daphne Nelson and her son. Some facts have been discovered, and I'm hoping Martin can verify them."

"Which are?" Peal's eyes are ash-gray, only a shade or two away from being white. I see he likes to stare at people with them.

I return his gaze and answer, "The facts are in regards to an accident case your son handled some years ago. It involved the death of over sixteen people."

"Yes, the church bus case. It was a sad day in our community. That case helped me to understand Randolph's determination to become a personal-injury attorney; seeing the vigor he drew on to pursue adequate settlements for all those families. I was proud of the boy."

His eyes cast to the left when he says he was "proud of the boy." I read somewhere that eye movement such as that meant lying. And hearing this European-looking African-American man say "our community" for the second time adds to my uneasiness.

This uneasiness bothers me because I realize my edginess with this brother is based on how he looks. I am prejudging him by appearance. A brother like me is being prejudiced, and not only that; I have yet to offer him my condolences. He has lost a son.

A pain I am all too familiar with, and I have allowed my

own prejudice to stop me from being a compassionate person. Because he is a black man who looks white, I have held back my concern.

"Mr. Peal, please accept our sympathies for the loss of your son." I included Ricky, who nods his head in agreement.

"Thank you, Mr. Price. Randolph and I . . . our relationship was strained, to say the least. You see, his mother and I never married. We were college lovers. She and her parents raised Randolph. He was an adult before he came into my life and the life of my other sons. My wife Helen opened our family to him, but he had issues. He never felt a part of my family, and I understood. Even though I gave him my name at birth, his mother's parents insisted on raising him without assistance from me, and at that time any assistance from me wouldn't have amounted to much.

"An African-American man of my complexion is not always accepted by our community. I could have practiced as a white man, but I chose to be part of the community I was born in. I advised Randolph to do the same. He took my advice for ostracism. It wasn't.

"I believed it would have been easier for him to practice as a white attorney in mainstream society. When one looked at Randolph, no traces of his African-American heritage were seen. He was not born in or raised in our community. Randolph Peal by anyone's standard was a white man.

"When he finished law school he wanted to join my firm. My partner and my sons were against it. You see, Mr. Brown, Mr. Price, we have worked for our reputation within the community and my sons have worked hard to make sure that we are thought of as an African-American firm; our practice targets mid- to upper-income African-Americans.

"You see I was stuck between one son wanting to be involved in his father's career and three sons who thought his involvement would hurt us all. My solution was to become a silent partner with Randolph. He took my money, but not my advice. He targeted his practice at our community."

Ricky says, "It seemed to have worked for him."

"Yes, he proved me wrong. Randolph's firm was profitable after the first year. People in the community trusted him, especially after the church bus tragedy. Randolph's clients viewed him as a white man and they accepted him as such. After the bus tragedy, the sky was the limit for this firm.

"Mr. Price, how is that terrible tragedy linked to the death of Ms. Nelson and her son?"

"What I have, Mr. Peal, is a hypothesis, one that I am not at liberty to share."

"I see. Is what you're doing related at all to my son's murder?"

"Yes, I believe it is."

"Who has employed your services?"

"Ms. Nelson was a dear friend, and she died on my porch. I am doing this on my own."

"Understandable."

Martin enters pushing a cart with sandwiches and coffee. The senior Peal stands, takes a sandwich and walks to the door, "Martin, these gentlemen would like to speak to you in private. I am going down to Accounting. Buzz me when you're finished here. And again, Mr. Price and Mr. Brown, it was a pleasure. And please keep my firm in mind for any of your estate or tax needs." He closes the door behind him.

Martin pours himself a cup of coffee, grabs a sandwich,

and takes the seat behind the desk. Ricky doesn't hesitate to take two sandwiches and a bottle of water. He passes me a sandwich and bottle of water.

I want to get right into Martin, so without hesitating I ask, "Was Mr. Peal always involved in the day-to-day operations before Randolph's death?"

"No, this morning at six-thirty AM was the first time I've met the man. I usually don't work on Wednesdays," he says with much attitude.

"This clown picked me up at my home and brought me to work. He introduced himself by telling me Randolph was dead and I should be at work." Martin bites into the sandwich and gulps the coffee. "I feel like I am being bullied. He sat in my living room while I showered and got dressed for work. He drove me in and told me I could expect to be here late tonight.

"The man has made it quite clear whose firm this is. Daphne was right; we were not Randolph's partners. This firm belongs to that man."

I have no sympathy for his employment situation. "When did you hear about Daphne?"

"I heard about it last night on the news. I didn't believe it. I called her house anyway and left a message . . ." He only eats half the ham sandwich, wraps up what's left in a napkin and tosses it in the wastebasket on the side of the desk. He does finish the coffee. "And the rumors around here are that he is black. Can you believe that?" He moved right past Daphne's death to his present situation.

"I believe Randolph killed Daphne."

"I thought the same, until he came up dead. Shot on *your* wife's back porch. How about that, Mr. Price?"

"Yeah, how about it?"

"What did the police say to you?" Martin asks, standing

and getting himself another sandwich and a bottle of water.

"Not much, why?"

He drops back down in the chair. "Because, man, you have to be the main suspect. No one else threatened Randolph's life and put a gun to his head. One can only hope that the police have at least spoken to you." He splits the second sandwich—tuna—in half and bites into it just as hungrily.

"Does Peal's father know about the altercation between Randolph and me?"

"Oh yes, I told him as soon as the receptionist said you were in the lobby."

Peal Senior is indeed a clever sort; there is no way I couldn't have held a conversation with the man who threatened my murdered son with a pistol, unless of course I didn't care about my son.

"Tell me, Martin, did you tell him about yourself?"

"What about me?" He twisted the water bottle open and swallowed.

"You know, man, about your father."

"My father?" When he looks up, surprise is all over his clean-shaven narrow face.

"Yeah, you know about Daphne and Randolph setting up the accident that ruined his business and caused him to kill himself."

He wags his finger at me, "Oh . . . that's why you wanted to see me. You're trying to piece together a motive for my involvement in Randolph's death. Mr. Price, save the effort for your own defense. You'll need it." He starts chuckling and twists the cap back on the water.

"My father was a sick man before the accident, a weak man who suffered from major depression. I didn't blame

Randolph or Daphne. I doubt if Randolph or Daphne even knew who my father was. They sued Aspire Trucking, not Matthew MacNard. My father was never named in the suit.

"Aspire Trucking was a franchise owned by the bank, not my father. Gentlemen, you are aware that Aspire Trucking is a national franchise; which was the reason Randolph was able to get such large settlements?"

I wasn't familiar with Aspire's business status, and neither was Ricky.

"Judging by the expressions on your faces, you two bros didn't know Aspire was national? Tsk, tsk. Do your homework, gentlemen."

No one likes to be showed up; Ricky likes it less than most. He leans up to the edge of the couch cushion. "You tellin' us that y'all never spoke of ya daddy's death?"

"No. I didn't see a need." Martin reminds me of a turtle with his head stretched out from the shell.

"You was wokin' fo' da man dat killed ya daddy?"

Smiling and as condescending as hell, Martin continues with, "Sir, you share the same mistaken belief that my mother had. No law firm killed my father. My father killed himself. I am a thirty-three-year old partner in the city's top-billing personal injury firm, and for the record, Mr. Brown, if this firm had been responsible for the death of my father, I'd still be here."

I believe him, and Ricky must too because he sits back.

"What about Daphne?" I ask.

"What about her, Mr. Price? She's dead. She had a great rack, a tight little ass and wonderful feet . . . I'll tell you something . . . she was the first black woman I ever dated. Usually all they can do for me is point me in the direction of a white one. But Daphne had ambition. Her ambition almost rivaled mine. We had our good moments, but my world will not be slowed by her demise."

The young man is sick, and sick people should be helped. I want to tell him something that will help him, but I hear Ricky saying, "Nigga, you fucked in da head."

And that pretty much ends our visit. Martin springs up from his chair and shows us the door. I pull a card from my wallet and hand it to him. He doesn't tear it up. Leaving I ask, "Hey, do you know anyone who drives a white Bentley?" My card slips from his hand.

"No," he answers and bends down for my card.

Now I understand why Eleanor asked me if I had met Randolph's father. That was her way of telling me that Randolph had some African-American heritage, as slight as it was. I follow Ricky out the offices of Zonderman, Peal and MacNard. Daphne's plastic letters had been taken down.

I cannot align my thoughts. I now know that Peal's daddy is an African-American, Martin is a total sell-out, Eleanor wants to meet again, Regina wants me locked up and the cops think I'm a murderer. All these thoughts add up to . . . nothing. I don't have a clue as to who killed Daphne, Stanley or Peal or who the hell was in that white Bentley.

Back in his truck, Ricky reminds me that I need to go see Daphne's parents.

# Chapter Fourteen

When we get out to Harvey, Mr. Nelson is standing in his front yard in the shade of his huge oak tree. He stops nailing the HOUSE FOR SALE sign in the ground and greets me. He's solemn upon approach but accepts my hug. Dressed in a pair of green work pants and thick black suspenders over a V-neck T-shirt, he directs me inside the house.

In the kitchen I greet old neighbors and walk up on Regina, toting her customary tuna casserole. We nod to each other and turn away. I walk into the dining room to get a seat and notice a picture of Daphne and Eleanor on the mantle.

They look like happy sisters hugged up cheek to cheek. It's a very recent photo. In the background of the photograph, I notice a black DTS Caddy across the street. At first glance I think it's mine, but Daphne's parents live behind Regina's house. They share an alley. Most of the time my car is parked in front of Regina's house. The DTS in the picture can't be mine.

As Mr. Nelson walks in through the front door, I ask him

about the owner of the car in the photo. He tells me Martin, Daphne's boyfriend. I'm about to ask him a couple of questions, but his eyes tear up. He grabs a hold of my arm and pulls me into a bedroom. I guess it belongs to him and his wife.

He stands right up on me and says, "She was a good girl, Mr. Price. Her and Stanley didn't deserve to get shot down like dogs in the street. Everything she did wasn't right, but people make mistakes. What her and that white lawyer was doing wasn't a secret to me. She called me yesterday and told me she was going to tell you. She trusted you, Mr. Price, always did.

"When that white lawyer got her that first big check, my little girl was hooked. There was nothing me or her mama could say to turn her around. The money talked to her louder than we did. But something was happening with her here lately. I think she was starting to see that some things are better than money.

"Last month she started talking different. She was regretting things she had done. She told her mama and me about the bus accident. We prayed for her and told her to pray. Our God is a forgiving God. I told her all she had to do was ask and He would forgive her. But it wasn't God she was afraid of; it was that white lawyer. She thought he would hurt her if she told people what happened."

Mr. Nelson is standing right in my face and it's getting uncomfortable. I take a step back, and for clarification I ask, "Are you talking about Randolph Peal?"

"Yeah, he was the devil who worried her. You see, Mr. Price, Daphne didn't want Stanley involved in that crooked business. But she didn't know how to stop it from happening. She started bringing him around here, hoping I could tell him something. But young men looking for riches don't listen to their poor granddaddies.

"But I thank the Lord she brought him around here those last couple of months; at least I got to know him and her again. She would even bring her friend Eleanor by from time to time. That picture on the mantle is from a little birthday thing she had over here for Eleanor. Boy, we played some dominos that day! I even got that uppity boyfriend of hers to play a game.

"At first I didn't believe the boy was from Chicago. He was too white-acting to be from around here. Some of us may put on airs around white folks, but very few of us put on airs around each other. That boy kept putting on. It wasn't until I found that I knew his daddy did I believe he was from around here."

"You knew Matthew MacNard."

"We were lodge brothers. He was a good-natured man, always a kind word."

"Really? I heard he was a melancholy type of man."

"No! Not Matthew. He loved life. He was the chairman of the entertainment committee. A robust man, he was. He loved new Cadillacs and fat Cuban cigars. Martin driving that Caddy is the only thing about him that reminds me of his father. Matthew MacNard enjoyed life and he had a good one, until that tragic bus accident. It ruined him.

"He couldn't come back after it happened. He held himself responsible because the brakes on one of the trucks failed. He must have told me a hundred times how he fixed the truck's brakes that morning.

"People say Matthew killed himself because he lost his business. Hell, it was a two-truck business and he drove one of the trucks. No. He killed himself out of guilt. You see he lied and told the company he was getting them trucks fixed at a shop, but he wasn't. Matthew would keep all the repair money and work on the trucks himself. It was guilt that drove him to eat a bullet.

"But then I come to find out it wasn't the truck's fault, and the whole thing was a setup, a phony accident to make some money. And here this man now went and killed himself. If it was anybody's fault, it was the lawyer's. He set the crooked mess up, him and . . . my baby . . . But it was him, that white lawyer who led her down that sinful path.

"Ain't no justice in this world, Mr. Price. I learned that when I came back from Korea. A poor man ain't gonna never get his due, not from man, anyhow. It was wrong that Matthew and all them people on the bus had to die so that lawyer could make some money, and it was wrong that my daughter and her son got shot down to keep his secret safe. And that's what I think happened. She wanted out of that business, but he wouldn't let her go that easy. She probably threatened to go to the police, so he her killed.

"The quick and the dead, the good Lord judges them both, Mr. Price. We might get past man's law, but there is no getting by the Father. And I find my comfort in knowing that *that* moneychanger is being dealt with by my Father.

"Mr. Price. I know you remember when the drink had control of my life. It wasn't a secret that things weren't getting done for my family. There was no fatherly guidance in this house for my daughter or my grandson.

"Other people in the neighborhood spent time with them. Mrs. Coleson, bless her soul, took Daphne with her up to New York every summer, and you with Stanley. I remember him bursting out our back gate running over to your house. He couldn't wait to spend time with you. As soon as he got off the school bus he was headed to your yard.

"What I'm trying to do, Mr. Price, is thank you for the time you spent with my grandson. You was there for him when his grandfather wasn't, and for that I thank you." He gives me a quick awkward hug.

"I'm moving come week's end. Me and the missus are headed back home to Alabama. We going to bury Daphne and the boy in our family plot. I'm through with up here. We were planning on going down next year, but there is no sense in putting it off any longer. It's time to take these old bones south."

I nod my head but say nothing. We shake hands and walk back into the living room. I look for Mrs. Nelson to offer my condolences, but before I can find her, I notice a gathering of neighborhood ladies staring at me, and none of the looks are friendly. The group opens a little and I see Regina is in the middle of the crowd. Suddenly I feel closed in and decide it's time to leave.

Climbing into Ricky's truck, I'm engulfed by a cloud of weed smoke. He must have smoked a heck of a lot to have a cloud this dense; especially since the air conditioner is on full blast. He passes me the joint. I decline because getting high redirects and slows my thoughts. Ricky claims smoking weed targets his thinking and allows him to concentrate. I doubt it.

"D, I was thinkin' we should put Eleanor, Martin and Peal's daddy together. I'm thinkin' Peal's daddy is a suspect too. I didn't trust him fo' a minute. He up in there taking over his son's business and the man ain't been dead a day."

Waving the smoke from my face, I say, "He told us he was a silent partner. I kind of trust the man." Who I didn't trust was Martin and Eleanor. Ricky's earlier thought about them being in cahoots was starting to make sense to me.

"What! If you trust dat guy you in over ya head." Ricky takes a long, deep hit from the joint. The cloud he exhales is huge. "Didn't Martin say that they was da top-billin' personal-injury firm in da city?"

"Yep."

"Dat's got to be a lot of money. Now da daddy gets it all." He hit the joint hard and exhaled another dense cloud.

Maybe I'm getting a contact high because Ricky's point seems valid. He tries to pass me the joint again. This time I take it and hit it. While I'm exhaling my own cloud, Regina starts tapping on Ricky's driver window. He flips the power button and the window rolls down, letting free a boulder of weed smoke.

Regina fans the smoke out of her face and says, "I know damn well you two are not sitting out here getting high in front of these people's house! They just lost their daughter and grandchild! You are not that insensitive, are you, Ricky?"

Ricky's sitting there looking at her with his mouth hanging open, saying nothing. She's coming at him too fast. I know his brain is overloading. He wants to say something but he can't. I can't help him, after hitting the joint . . . I'm stuck too.

"You are two ignorant-ass motherfuckers!" She turns and walks away heels with clicking on the sidewalk.

I was going to go see Chester, but not now . . . I hit the joint again. Ricky is looking at Regina walking back to the house. He starts the truck and I hit the joint again.

"Man, give me my damn joint!"

I want to pass it to him, but my arm won't move in his direction. Matter of fact, my arm is not moving at all.

Ricky turns his globe of a head to me, and he looks worried. "Damn, I forgot ya ass hardly smoke weed. Dat shit is too potent for you. Dat's dat hydro, baby!" His worried frown changes to a grin. "How you feelin'?"

Like I'm stuck is what I want to tell him, but talking is out of the question. I force my arm to pass Ricky the joint. Something is wrong with me. If it wasn't for seeing the passing houses I would not know the truck is moving. It feels like I'm stuck in a hole full of heavy mud. I don't like this here feeling at all. This situation calls for closed eyes, I didn't get any good sleep last night; maybe it's time to try again. Smoking weed has really never been my thing. I can remember the first time Ricky and I tried it.

We were in my grandmother's backyard at the brick barbecue pit in the middle of her yard. Ricky had the matches and I had the "punks," brown incense sticks that supposedly keep the mosquitoes away, but we used them to act like we were smoking joints. We held them between our thumb and index finger and made the hissing, inhaling noise of those who smoked weed.

This hot afternoon, however, we were using them to burn the spiders we found in the corners of my grandmother's brick pit. We thought it amazing that the spiders would wrap their legs around the incense sticks, while the hot tip was burning through them. We'd killed about five, and the game wasn't getting boring at all. This was better than dropping lit matches on ants.

My older brothers, Charles and Robert, were on the upstairs back porch looking down at us. They were drinking the remains of a case of Schlitz that my uncle had left after the Fourth of July celebration. And they were also getting high smoking green weed.

Commercial is what they called the weed, and they weren't happy about having to smoke it. Columbian or "Bo" had just arrived in our neighborhood, but it cost ten dollars. And Mama left them the same amount of money she left Ricky and me: five dollars. We were all supposed to go to Taurus Flavors and get ice cream and steak sandwiches.

They wanted "Bo," me and Ricky wanted Taurus Flavors, and at eleven years of age, armed with screwdrivers and sticks, we were keeping our five dollars. We thought they were stupid; why smoke something on a hot day when you could sit inside the air-conditioned Taurus Flavors and eat a steak sandwich and ice cream? We wasn't going for it, so they had to get commercial instead of "Bo."

Ricky and I were so engrossed in our hunt for another spider we didn't see them come down the stairs. "Man, what you lames doing?" Charles asked.

"Killing," Ricky said.

"Killing what?"

"Spiders," I told him.

Robert asked, "Why?"

"'Cause they hold on, even after they got a hole burned through them," I told him.

"Man that's some lame little-kid stuff. When y'all gonna start actin' cool? Y'all gonna be in fifth grade next year; that's too old to be killing bugs. That ain't cool."

We pulled our heads from the pit and stopped immediately. They pulled us in by using the dreaded phrase of any eleven-year-old kid, "It ain't cool."

After all, they were the big brothers. They understood cool. They wore Chuck Taylor All Star gym shoes, pressed khaki pants and silk T-shirts. Their Afros were so big they used rakes, not picks. They rode five-speed polo bikes with steering wheel handlebars and sissy poles. They knew whole Richard Pryor albums and had done "it" to girls. If they said something "ain't cool," it wasn't.

"Here, drink these and come on over here in the shade with us."

The four of us stood in the shade of my grandmother's crab apple tree with Shlitz cans in hand. My brothers drank theirs while Ricky and I held ours. We'd tasted beer and we didn't like it. Ricky's mother's Boone's Farm wine was much better.

"Man, why y'all standing there like some lames holding them cans? Here, do it like this." My brother Robert opened another can and downed it in three gulps. "That's how you do it. Now y'all try, see how many swallows it takes you."

We had only tasted Boone's Farm wine and beer. We had never gulped either. And gulping with the purpose of finding out how many gulps it took to empty a can motivated us through four cans a piece.

Robert lit a joint and began smoking it. Ricky and I watched him out the corner of our eyes. I wanted to smoke some as long as it didn't cost us our five dollars. Robert called me to him. He put the joint inside his mouth backwards, cupped his hands around my nose and mouth and blew smoke into me. He did the same to Ricky. We both bent over and gagged. When we finished coughing I looked over at Ricky to see if he looked any different. He didn't. And I didn't feel any different except for the beer bubbling in my stomach.

Charles passed us a bottle of some stuff that looked like water. I knew it wasn't water by the smell, but we drank it anyway. It was gin, and we promptly threw up all that was inside our stomachs. While we were bent over regurgitating, my brothers went through our pockets and took the five dollars.

When my grandmother got home from her part-time job at the alderman's office, she found us passed out drunk under the crab apple tree. She pieced together what happened from our slurred answers.

All my childhood life, Grandma had threatened to get me with the razor strap that hung on her bathroom door, but it never came off the hook for me. My brothers told me of the horrible beatings they received from it, and that was enough to stop me from being too bad over Grandma's. Obviously my brothers had forgotten about the strap.

With the strap in her pocketbook she walked Ricky and me to Taurus Flavors. There in the air-conditioned restaurant sat my brothers, eating steak sandwiches and ice cream. I didn't think grandma was going to go in there and beat them in front of the man who owned the store, but she did.

At the time my grandmother was bigger than both of my brothers. So when they tried to stand up she shoved them back down in the booth. She was hitting them hard with that strap and harder with words.

She told them God cursed people who taught little kids how to sin, and she couldn't figure out how "chilrens" so evil could be part of her. When she finished beating them she dragged them home by the back of their shirts. Needless to say, that sight didn't help their "cool" image a bit. It took years for kids in our neighborhood to stop talking about it.

Once home, she made them cut the front and back grass with her rusty old push mower, and they had to edge the grass with butcher knives. That evening she fried me and Ricky pork chops, but the best part was, she got her ice-cream maker out and made my brothers churn it, but me and Ricky got all the custard.

I haven't dreamed about my grandmother in a while. It's been even longer since I've dreamed of my childhood.

When I open my eyes, I see white and pink suds cover the windows of Ricky's truck. We're in a car wash. Ricky is sipping on an iced cappuccino. I spot one in the cup holder for me.

" 'Bout time you woke up. You been out for over two hours. I now went and bought a city sticker, made a bank drop and picked up some souse."

"Souse? You got crackers?"

"Yeah in the back seat in da bag with da souse. Ain't but a pound, don't find a home in it."

The souse meat is in deli paper. That meant he drove all the way down 51st Street to get it. I been 'sleep awhile. He's got some pepper cheese in the bag also. I take a slice of souse and cheese and fold them both between the crackers.

"D, I don't think you gonna get to the bottom of dis here mess. Ya dealing with some rich, powerful, wicked motherfuckers who don't care 'bout killing they own. I think Peal's daddy did it all. Think about it, man. Peal wasn't a killer. You made him piss in his pants.

"Yeah, at first thought I went with Peal, but man, dis was some cold, calculated shit. Dis was cleanin' up da loose ends. And Peal was a loose end. I think the daddy found out the bus was a hooked-up accident and tripped. He couldn't afford to be associated with dat type of disaster. I mean dis man does work for the Reverend Jesse Jackson. He cain't be involved in no lowlife accident cases. You feel me?"

What I was feeling was another souse, cheese and cracker sandwich, so I reached to the back and quickly made me another one.

"Ricky, you talking about this man killing his son. And for what, money? He's already rich." Jet streams of water are spraying the truck.

"Man, rich white people kill each other over money all da time. They ain't never rich enough."

"You forgetting Ricky, they're not white." Ricky reaches into the back seat and folded up the souse, cheese and crackers. I guess that's it for the snacks. I grab the cup of cappuccino and blow the foam from the top and drink.

"They look white and they white rich."

"What the hell is 'white rich'?"

"You know, white people rich, real money."

"Ricky, you are worth what, five, six million?"

"Huh?"

"I'm asking your net worth, between the properties, the liquor stores, the cleaning business, I know it's over five million."

"So, what's ya point?"

"You are 'white people rich,' if one chooses to use that phrase. Most white people don't have the money you have. I guarantee you Peal's daddy isn't as rich as you. Man, we as a people have got to stop putting ourselves beneath white people!"

"Man I ain't putting no white man over me!"

"You just did it, 'white people money, real money' . . . Your money is real. You earned it . . . It's just as good as theirs. 'White people rich,' please."

I could tell Ricky is thinking about what I'm saying because he's gotten quiet.

"It's closer to ten."

"What?"

"My net worth, it's closer to ten million. Dat's da reason Martha been sweatin' me about movin' out of da city. She say we can afford to live better dan we do."

"Ten million? Damn man, I'm with Martha! It's time to move, boss."

"Yeah, well, whatever. But back to Peal, I still say he didn't care about his weakest-link son. And ya missed da point, he didn't kill him fo' money. He killed him so da fallout from da bus thang wouldn't come back to him.

"I think dat Peal called up his daddy and told him about da threat Daphne had become. The daddy figured it would only be a matter of time before he was connected to it all."

"But Ricky, all he did was invest money. A father can help a son. And Martin told us Peal Senior wasn't part of the day to day; he would have no problem proving that. His son ran the firm, not him."

Ignoring me, Ricky says, "I'm gonna tell you what happened. He gave Randolph a couple of dollars to get started. Den all of a sudden da boy started makin' money. Daddy Peal starts thinkin' if da reject son can make money from dis, he knew one of his real boys would turn it out."

"I know you're not thinking he killed his white son to put one of his black ones charge of the firm." Ricky must have got a super-wash because the sudsy brushes are back on the windows.

"Yeah, dat's what I'm thinkin' exactly."

"Ricky, my brother, it's time for you to quit smoking weed. Please let it go, partner . . . Just let it go." The jet streams of water return are giving the illusion of movement.

"Okay, make fun if you want to, but we will see."

"Yeah man, we will see."

After the truck is air-blown dry, we pull onto the busy Torrence Avenue. I'm shocked to see that we are in Calumet City; I thought we were still on the south side. But I should have known because the gas stations out in the suburbs amaze me; you can fill up, get your car washed, get a fast-food meal and gourmet-style coffee.

I glance in the passenger mirror on the door and spot a detective car lit up and gaining.

"Ricky, pull over, man, I think the police are going to need to get by us."

"Oh shit! Man, dump that ashtray out the window! Dem cops ain't trying' to go by us, they coming fo' us!"

As I dump the ashtray, the cops speed past. I look at Ricky, whose eyes are glued to the fading detective's car.

"I told you man . . . Just let it go, paranoia is one of the signs. You been smoking that stuff too long."

Ricky blows a heavy sigh and relaxes back in his seat. "Man where you want me to take ya because I'm 'bout gettin' tired of yo ass."

"Irritability is another sign."

"Look-a-here, man, enough is enough. Now where we goin'?"

"Well you in this with me, where do you think I should go next?"

"I came out to the south 'burbs while you was passed out, because I was thinkin' Eleanor's was the next move. Now I could be wrong since I'm on da verge of some type of marijuana-induced breakdown." He lets go of the steering wheel and starts trembling his upper torso.

"That ain't funny, man. You wouldn't be the first man who baked his brain on weed. And I wasn't passed out, I was 'sleep, But you're right, Eleanor's is our next stop."

# Chapter Fifteen

Ricky has replaced Howlin' Wolf with Buddy Guy and I'm seriously grooving to Buddy's guitar licks. My cell phone rings. Ricky frowns, but turns the music down; it's Carol updating me. She gives me the Nelsons' phone number, which I no longer need, and next she tells me that the police called and my Caddy was stolen from the impound lot.

I hear her telling me to stay calm. I tell her I will and ask is there anything else. She says no and clicks off the line.

There is nothing I can do about my Caddy. I am not going to drive around looking for it and I'm ninety-eight percent certain the police are not going to pay for it.

"What's up, D?"

"My Caddy got stolen from the police impound."

"Damn, now dat's a bold car thief. Will da city pay for it?"

"I'm reporting it to my insurance company. They can deal with the city. The car is insured against theft. It was stolen. Where it was stolen from and who stole it is not my problem."

"I hear you. Get whatcha pay fo', bro."

"Did I tell you Mr. Nelson said Martin drives a Black DTS like mine?"

"Naw . . . Well damn man . . . dat's who me and Gina saw peeling out da alley! Remember she was screamin' to the police about seein' you leavin' da alley!"

"You right, my baked-brain brother, and that explains how Peal got out to Regina's. When the police arrested me I didn't see his SUV anywhere in sight. I was wondering how the hell he got out there. He rode with Martin. I saw him and Martin climb in the SUV, but I didn't see them drive off. Wait a minute, let's go over Daphne's place. I want to see if Peal's SUV is still parked there. If it is, we got Martin."

"How?"

"Yesterday Martin set up a meeting with Daphne to draw her out the house so Peal could break in and get files on the bus accident. We got back to Daphne's before Peal had a chance to leave and caught him easing out. Stanley beat him down. Martin comes out of nowhere and helps Peal. But this is the kicker—after the whipping Peal took he couldn't have driven. That puts him and Martin in the car together. If Peal's BMW SUV is there, it's bye-bye, Martin."

Ricky nods his head agreeing, "Yeah man, you on to something now." He turns the volume on Buddy Guy back up and heads for 94 Westbound.

Cruising by the new houses on Clark, Ricky says "Maybe Martha will be happy living down here."

"No, I don't think so. Martha wants a full spread, dude, and you know it; gated-community living or on a golf course.

You got it like that, Ricky. Don't be afraid to live at your station. When we get out to Eleanor's take a look around. Out there is where a man worth ten million should have his family."

No sooner do we enter the guest lot than I see Peal's SUV. "There it is. Pull alongside it, man."

Ricky parks and we both jump out and walk around the BMW. We start looking in the windows for what I don't know. I flip my cell open to call the police when I feel it. There is a pistol in my back. I look over and see Ricky collapse.

"I told you we would get to dance!"

I try to turn but I'm going down too, from a hard knock on the head.

What wakes me up is the smell of sewage. Ricky and I are gagged and bound to wooden blocks in a dim, damp basement. Shadows are swaying on the wall in front of us. The light must be hanging above us. Behind me I hear voices, all males.

"Why did you bring them here?"

"I didn't know what you wanted me to do with them. The fat one's Ricky Brown; he's worth a handsome ransom."

"And what does that have to do with me? All I wanted you to do was make the BMW disappear."

"We make people disappear, geek, not trucks."

I'm guessing it's about three people behind us.

"Yes, I saw how well you make people disappear, especially innocent people."

I'll be damned; it's Martin.

"That bitch wasn't innocent, little brother, and her little mark-ass son was doin' the same shit that fucked up our lives, so he wasn't innocent either."

"We all agreed to ruin Peal."

"Naw that's you and Lady with all that plannin' shit. I told y'all two years ago when I got out all they asses was goin' down. The guilty will be fallin'!"

"These men are not guilty."

"Naw they ain't, so what do you want us to do with them?"

"Let them go."

"Not today, and you know what . . ."

Three shots are fired.

I look over to Ricky, he's fine. My head is ringing. The shots sounded incredibly loud. The basement must be small.

"Damn, Mac . . . You shot your brother all to shit! Why you do that?"

"I'm not my brother's keeper . . . The motherfucker just wasn't actin' right. Especially after he found out I popped his bitch. He didn't want the slut responsible for his own daddy and mama dyin', dead. We went homeless after my daddy died and the bitch he was fucking was part of the reason.

"Him and Lady have gotten soft with money. He was too weak to trust. It was only a matter of time before he turned me over to the cops."

"But MacKnock, he did shoot the lawyer."

"No he didn't. He said he didn't do it. He asked me did I open fire on him and the lawyer. He said the two of them was on the back porch together and all of a sudden somebody started shooting at them. Martin didn't kill the damn lawyer. His punk ass thought it was me shooting at them. The motherfucker was too scared and paranoid. He didn't pop that lawyer."

"Damn, well who did the lawyer?"

"I don't know and don't give a fuck, I'm just glad his ass is dead."

"What about them two?"

"We holdin' they ass for ransom. Get in touch with Ricky Brown's people; them niggas are hip to the ransom game. Hey, grab they watches and wallets so they people will know we fo' real. If they don't pay, we can bury they ass right down here with the rest of the marks."

My Rolex is snatched from my wrist and he cuts open my jeans to take the wallet.

"MacKnock, didn't you say you wanted to get with this cat here?"

"Later. I got to get the Bentley back out to Lady and the BMW and the Ford to the chop shop. His ass ain't goin' nowhere."

The light goes out and we hear them climbing stairs. A door is slammed shut and a bolt clanks in its holder. Damn, it's dark. A minute or so later I hear a big engine turn over. It can't be fifteen feet away. A heavy bass beat follows the engine starting. We hear the vehicle pull off.

Ricky tries several times to stand, and so do I. We are bound to the wooden blocks. The way we are taped and tied it's useless to struggle, but we both keep trying. I hear Ricky tumble over. He stops moving. I can't call to him. I cease my own movement and hold my breath, straining to hear anything from him. A fatigued groan comes from his direction.

Ricky's to the right, but to my left where the engine noise came from I hear a rumbling. Now it's thuds; someone is kicking against something. It's the window. The window is kicked open and the evening light comes through.

A kid scoots through the window with a flashlight. He makes a birdlike call and the basement door is shot open. Two kids come through it with pistols and knives. They cut us free and help us up. I run to Martin and check his pulse. He's gone. One of the kids is pulling me out the basement door. Thank you, Jesus!

We are hurried into a wrecked but drivable '98 Oldsmobile. JT,.Stanley's problem slides behind the wheel and floors the big sedan.

"We seen them grab y'all," he yells excitedly. "Them niggas don't play. If they wouldna left, it wouldna been shit we coulda did to get y'all out of there 'cept call the police. Them niggas is killers fo' real. Big MacKnock and his boy be about makin' folks disappear off the face of the earth.

"We heard about Snap and his mama on the news. We was drivin' over there to get some information about the services and saw them jackin' y'all.

"Man, Mr. Brown! I know we all hired for that management training program now! I want to get started tomorrow and I want to be in a store way out in the suburbs, away from all this drama!"

Ricky has JT and his crew drop him at home. He is quiet and reserved during the ride to his house. Seeing him this calm after being held hostage is spooky. He tells the boys to call him in the morning about the training program. He barely says goodbye to me.

I'm expecting him to try and convince me to ride with him to find the kidnappers. He doesn't. He tells me not to report anything to the police. He leaves me in the car with JT and his crew.

I have Ricky's future store managers drop me off at my office. I don't want to go home; I need to think, and my office is the best place for that. Besides, going home will get me back on Daphne and Stanley. I'm going to miss them both, not from the past but from the time we just spent together. Mr. Nelson was right; they didn't deserve to get shot down like rabid dogs, but the truth of it is . . . Matthew MacNard didn't deserve what Daphne and Peal did to him either.

In the bottom drawer of my old-fashioned desk is a gallon of E&J brandy. I seldom drink E&J nowadays, but a client whose mother we helped get her Medicaid remembered when I did.

The lights in the office are on. I guess Carol had to hurry home. I drop down in my swivel chair, retrieve the gallon and fill my coffee cup to the brim. It's not Remy but it will do. Gulping the brandy, I don't hear her until she says, "Boss, I thought you stopped drinking like that."

Usually Carol sneaking up on me in this fashion would have startled me. But I do believe being bound in the basement has worn out all my fear indicators, and I am entirely too tired to get startled. I keep drinking until my cup is empty.

Carol shakes her head, stops at my desk, bends down and gives me a quick peck on my forehead. "Are you okay, D?"

"Everything is fine, just a little tired." I lie to her because me talking ain't happening.

"If you have any questions about the stuff on your desk, call me. I got a hair appointment on 91st and Ashland so I'll be close for a while. Oh, . . . and, boss," she pinches her nose closed and informs me, "you got an odor on you. Take care of that fast." She floats right out the door.

"Okay." I say to her back.

On my desk is information on the MacNard family. It starts with an article about Matthew MacNard's suicide. Martin's older brother Michael found him dead. The next article was about Mildred MacNard, who accidentally set herself on fire while smoking on a shelter cot. She died two days later. The last article is about Michael MacNard being convicted of assault against Attorney Randolph Peal.

Maybe if I had come to the office earlier, Martin might be alive. I could have confronted him about his lies and possibly found out about his twisted brother.

Two coffee cups full of E&J would be a bit too much. As I pour only half a cup of the brandy, the thought of calling the police on Michael MacNard enters my mind, despite Ricky's request. The murdering bastard should be in jail. I drink down the brandy.

I don't pour any more E&J because the band of stress that was wrapped tight around my head has been loosened. Drinking more will have me drunk. Instead of getting up and going home to feed my dogs, my fingers are dialing Eleanor's number. Michael answers.

When he hears my voice, he asks, "Mr. Price?"

"Yeah, MacKnock, it's me." He slams the phone down before I can tell him to turn himself into the police.

I call back and a woman answers. She tells me Eleanor is over Daphne's folks' house. I stand to go to my car and remember there is no car. I spot the Nelsons' phone number on Carol's desk. Eleanor is there, and she agrees to meet me at my office.

In the back room I keep a travel bag with an emergency outfit and toiletries. Carol was right; there is an odor about me. Standing in the men's room before the face bowl, smelling myself, my grandmother enters my thoughts.

I was about sixteen, and she'd gotten sick for the first time in my life. The doctor told her not to bathe, but she had me help her to the bathroom anyway: "Boy, a birdbath is better than no bath, and besides, ain't a place on my body I can't reach with a soapy towel. Being sick ain't no reason to be smelling, you smell yourself before anybody else can smell you."

When she called me back into the bathroom to help her back to her bed, she was smelling fresh. After she got propped up on her pillow and settled under her covers she gave me wink and said, "Nobody on God's good earth wants to be stinky."

It takes a couple of sinks full of water but I finally get the scent of the basement off of me. In my travel bag is a pair of jeans, briefs and a black oversized jersey. I hear a tap on the office door.

When Eleanor walks in she looks tired; she accepts my swivel chair, and I sit across the room at Carol's desk. Eleanor is wearing a very pretty pink linen dress. Slung over her shoulder is a straw bag purse. It seems like days ago that we sat in her garden.

"I've been getting repeated emergency pages from Michael. Why do I feel as if you have something to do with that, Mr. Price?"

"Why indeed?"

"Sorry?"

Niceties between her and I are over. She should receive an Oscar for her performance in the garden. She actually made me feel regretful for upsetting her. Eleanor knew Peal was involved in her mother's death, but like Martin, she let the wealth soothe her taste for retribution.

"How could you sit up in Daphne's parents' house, knowing what you do about the murders? Are you that heartless a person? You weren't raised to be an uncaring person, Eleanor. You come from good people, Eleanor, and we both know it."

"Daphne was my friend and so are her parents," she says in a snippy tone, trying to get defensive. "My going over there to pay my respects was the right thing to do. Daphne was my friend."

"What is Michael MacNard?" I ask hard.

"My houseman!" she snaps back.

Neither of us speak, I'm searching her face for sincerity or concern. Both are missing. What I see is nervousness.

Calmer, she says, "Mr. Price, Michael has been a troubled soul since his father's suicide."

"Troubled! Eleanor, he killed Daphne and Stanley, but you know this, right?"

"I didn't know when we spoke earlier, Mr. Price, I swear. Had I known, I would have turned him over to the police."

"Yeah, right. You can call the police now." I hold up the phone.

"No, I'm too involved now." She's fumbling through her bag avoiding my stare; she pulls out nothing and looks back up at me. "My aunt said he was getting stuff together to leave; perhaps he'll run."

I put the phone back in the cradle.

"Involved how?"

"Pardon?"

"How were you, Martin and Michael connected?"

She put her elbows on the desk, and drops her head into her palms. She rolls her eyes, looks up to the ceiling then back to me.

"Mrs. MacNard and my mother grew up together in the South Shore neighborhood. The three of us grew up like cousins. Even as children, Michael was the one always in trouble."

I put my hand up to stop her. "I'm not trying to hear about his troubled childhood."

"Mr. Price, ever since Michael's father died he's been hooked up in street mess: robbing people, selling drugs and even breaking into people's houses. Eventually he got hooked up with a crooked lawyer doing traffic accidents. Through these associations, he got wind of a rumor that his father's truck accident was a setup.

"Initially, Martin and I didn't believe, until we met the driver of the car. Once we discovered that he was a well-known crash expert, it was almost impossible to contain Michael. He wanted to kill Randolph and everyone involved.

"Martin convinced Michael that waiting would yield better results. He was in his second year of law school, and figured as a lawyer he could damage Randolph more. Daphne already had me in the firm, so my getting next to Randolph was no problem.

"Believe it or not, Randolph was guilt-ridden. Anything I asked that man for he gave me, but he took away the only person I really needed. I hated Randolph Peal, and I am happy he is dead.

"Martin allowed the money to take his focus. And I understood because we are the children of working-class parents, money at that level was a culture shock.

"He tried to persuade Michael against vengeance; well, actually, we both did. It didn't make sense to risk losing everything we had gained and were gaining for revenge.

"Michael didn't see it that way. He got tired of waiting and went after Randolph. He would have killed him if the police hadn't been in the restaurant that day. His promise to us was that when he got out of prison, everyone associated with the accident would die.

"Upon his release, Martin suggested he be my houseman. He did no work other than answering the door. The Bentley was pretty much his, and between me and Martin he had more than enough money to buy whatever he wanted. None of it was enough, he wanted them dead."

"Them?"

"Daphne and Peal."

"Wasn't Daphne your friend?"

"Yes, and I did everything I could to stop Michael. Martin and I begged him to let it go. He called us both sellouts and threatened us. I believe Martin is getting his nerve up to go to the police. Daphne's death hurt him."

"Martin is dead, baby. I was there for that one."

"Martin's dead?" I heard shock, but no sympathy.

"Yes."

"Are you going to call the police?"

"I can't; like you, I'm too involved."

"That means he is going to come after me next! He's killed Daphne, Martin and Randolph. Mr. Price, you have to protect me!"

"He didn't kill Randolph. I was kind of thinking you did that one."

"What? You need to stop playing. This is not a time for levity. Of course he killed Randolph, and he may come after you too."

She responded to my accusation too quickly to be guilty.

"No, he's not coming after me or you. He's running for his life."

She stands, but sits back down.

"Who is he running from? He's not scared of anyone. He's crazy."

Telling her about Ricky is pointless. Besides, how can I explain being aware of one black man hunting down another to kill, and doing nothing about it because the hunted one tied me up in a basement like a slaughter hog, threatened my life and took my Rolex? Would my explanation justify knowing of his impending death, and doing nothing?

What if my explanation included Daphne and Stanley's murder, would that vindicate my desire for Michael's death? No it wouldn't; but by not doing anything I might as well be pulling the trigger myself.

I see urgency in Eleanor's paper-bag brown face; the news of Martin's death has gotten her edgy. "Why are you sure he's running? He could be outside waiting for us!" She's up and pacing behind the desk. "Is this how you protected Daphne and Stanley? No wonder he got to them. Shouldn't you be up doing something?" She grabs her purse from the desk, and moves her pacing to the door. At the door she suddenly stops, turns and looks up at me, "Well come on! I need to go."

"The safest place for you is right here."

"You're kidding, right? We got to go to the police."

"What you say could connect you to the murders."

"Maybe, but we need protection. I'm going to the police!" She storms out the door. I guess she changed her mind about contracting my services.

I pick my phone and dial Ricky's cell. I've got to stop this Michael situation.

"What's up, D?" Ricky answers rapidly.

"I need you to come pick me up."

"No can do, bro. I'm in motion."

"Swing by."

"Cain't do it."

"Where are you?'

"About to see a man 'bout a dog."

The phone clicks off and I don't bother to call back. Maybe another cup full of brandy is not such a bad idea.

# Chapter Sixteen

I smell food. There is a McDonald's bag in my lap with two Quarter Pounders and a large fry. On my desk is the large drink. Ricky is here somewhere. I look on my wrist for my watch and remember it's gone. The clock next to the door reads one-thirty, the sun that is filling the office lets me know it's PM.

"What's up, man?" Ricky is walking up from the back in his stocking feet, jeans and his undershirt. I look across to Carol's desk and see his stuff; looks like he slept over there.

"Good morning. Where is Carol?"

"Ain't morning no mo'. Carol came in earlier and woke me up, but I fell back to sleep. I ain't seen her after dat." He bites into a Quarter Pounder.

"Did she try and wake me?"

"Naw, she said you needed to sleep."

"She must have the phones forwarded to her cell. Any of the other staff come in and see me like this?"

"Not that I know of."

"Cool. When did you get here?"

"Been with you since yesterday; you know what I'm sayin'." He looked at me hard with that sly grin on his face. "My truck got stolen from the Jewels lot down there on Roosevelt and Wabash. I called my manager from the Roosevelt and Ashland store. He gave us a ride to my house where I got my old Blazer. We went to the strip club out in Gary, got drunk and crashed here." He didn't even look up from his food while he gave me our alibi.

While unwrapping my own burger, I notice my Rolex and wallet on the desk. So much for MacKnock. Damn, part of me was hoping the police got to him before Ricky—not for his sake, but for Ricky's.

Ricky is trying to change his life, but I don't think a substantial change will happen if he continues to live by street rules. Rules of the street do not govern a normal life. It's the same for a square turning hustler: he can't bring his normal morals and rules to the street and expect to survive.

Ricky is not going to be able to take his hustler mentality into normal, everyday life and expect to survive either. He is going to have to become square, if he really wants to change. And Martha is right. It is time for them to move.

"It's time for you to move, Ricky."

"When I finish my sandwich, man, I'm up."

"No, man, I am not talking moving from here, I'm talking about your home."

"Oh yeah . . ." He pauses and looks up from his meal to me. "You right, last night kinda brought it right down front. Da love and respect niggas have fo' me ain't stronger than they need fo' money. MacKnock ain't da only nigga dat will see me as a payday. And I'm gettin' too old to do what it takes to deal with 'em . . . Hold up, let me say dat different.

"I am old enough not to want to do what it takes to deal with 'em. All MacKnock had in his crew was one guy, but what if they was ten or twenty deep? Dis shit coulda went on and on and on. The ransom game is gettin' strong out here. It's only a matter of time befo' a fool brings it to my family.

"Look-a-here, I ain't immune to gettin' got. And hungry hustlers are born every day. I have enough money to eliminate some of da danger. You right, it's time to move. But what about you?"

"What about me? I'm not as high-profile as you, my brother. I'm staying right where I am."

"Man, people know Gina's face. She in da paper every day. What a crook thank about grabbin' Chester ain't shit."

I hadn't thought about that; he's right.

"You grew up in da life just like me; we know the same type of people. You high-profile too. Jealous folks hate on you just like they hate on me. How many pistols you got on you? Normal people don't carry around pistols, D. Only shady folks. And don't even try dat escort shit, cause you was totin' pistols befo' you had da business. And in case you fo'got, bro, we got snatched workin' on yo stuff. It wasn't my business dat got us kidnapped, it was yours."

He's right on all points.

"Who we was ten fifteen years ago, don't mean jack to da young, hungry seventeen-year-old hustler. So you might as well go suburban house shoppin' with me." Saying that tickles him. He laughs so hard he chokes on his Quarter Pounder.

I never thought about living outside of Chicago. I love my hood and the people in it. That includes the hustlers, whores, shady folks, hardheaded youth, the squares and the church folks. I'm comfortable with them all, and as if he is reading my mind Ricky says, "It's like Martha said to me, to grow people got to get out of they comfort zone." He stuffs all the food wrappers into the bag and stands. "I gots to get on home. You want me to drop you off?"

Before I can answer him Regina walks in. She looks at both of us and doesn't say a word. She sits in the chair in front of my desk. She has on a gray business suit with a pink cotton shirt. Her tennis shoes are pink too.

Ricky sits back down, delaying his departure.

"I owe you an apology, David. Detective Lee called me at work. It appears Martin had a deranged brother. They found him and a friend both intoxicated out of their minds in Randolph's BMW truck. And poor Martin was found dead in the trunk of the truck. Johnny thinks . . ."

"Johnny?" I ask.

"Oh, I'm sorry—Detective Lee . . . he says the gun they found in the car with them was the same caliber as the one that killed Daphne and Stanley."

"What about Peal?" The question is to Regina, but my eyes are on the crooked smirk on Ricky's face.

"Yes, Detective Lee is confident that them being in possession of Randolph's truck, wallet and belongings will be enough to tie them to his murder as well. And Eleanor is relaying all the information concerning the bus accident." The smile that appears on her face interferes with her talking. "Oh . . . and I got the exclusive! It's running tomorrow on page three!"

She's doing a little tap dance while sitting in the chair. Ricky and I both start laughing, and I am happy for her.

"But, David, another part of why I stopped by is—I was wondering if you would like to keep Chester for me tonight?"

This woman has balls bigger than a bull. It is always about what she wants, when she wants it.

"What . . . you got plans already . . . so soon? Shouldn't you give yourself time to grieve over Randolph?"

She blows a heavy sigh and sucks her teeth. Then she turns to me and sets those will-weakening emerald eyes on me and asks, "What makes you think my plans aren't business?"

I flutter my own eyelashes, give a diva-imitating smile and say, " 'Cause I know you, Gina. You going out with the red Bob Marley tonight.

She crosses and uncrosses her thin legs. "Who? Never mind, can you or can't you keep Chester?"

I blow her a kiss and say, "Yes . . . I can. Who has him now?"

"My mother is watching him at the house."

"Can you drop me out there, Ricky?"

"You got it, bro."

Regina stands to leave. She looks as if she wants to say something, but changes her mind. What she says is, "I'll see you two later, and be careful. Whether you two know it or not, y'all getting too old for the streets." She hurries out of the office and I'll be damned if my eyes are not glued to her narrow hips. The truth be told, I still want me some of that.

I ask Ricky, "Why didn't you tell me, man?"

"Tell you what?"

"That Michael wasn't dead."

"If he was dead, I wouldn't tell ya. Why would I tell ya if I let him live?"

Again, he had a point.

"I just didn't feel killin' him, D. Yeah, he deserved it, but it wasn't in me. Instead we shot 'em full of enough dope to keep 'em confused for a couple of days, by den da police should be able to piece together somethin'.

"We caught up with 'em when they tried to sell da trucks; they took 'em to Fishback's shop. He called me soon as he saw my truck, even held 'em fo' me. I let him keep the Ford fo' da favor."

"I'm glad it turned out this way." I feel like doing my own happy dance.

"Me too, D . . . me too."

A small voice in the back of my head is asking me who killed Peal, but I hear another voice in my head. It's saying, "Fuck dat shyster."

While on the expressway heading out to Harvey to get Chester, Ricky has the Blazer cruising at around ninty-five miles per hour. Suddenly a long black car passes us like we are standing still, and it isn't shaking, rattling or swaying. It is swift.

"What was that?"

"That's that seven series Beamer, man."

"Damn, take me to get one."

When the salesman opens the door to the sedan all I can say is "Ohwee." After the test drive, Ricky and I are sold. When I see the sticker, "Damn" is all I can say. The walrus-looking sales-manager drops down two grand from the sticker and I write him a check for half the price of the car. Ricky trades the Blazer for his and writes a check for the remainder. He doesn't like car notes.

I guess the checks clear because the skinny manager brings out champagne and caviar. All I want is the manual, keys and a full tank of gas. They can keep the fish eggs.

After we finish the computer class they give on operating the vehicle, we are standing outside the dealership waiting for the porter to pull the sedans around. Ricky looks at me serious and asks, "Are you gonna go lookin' at houses with me and Martha?"

"Man, I ain't leaving Englewood."

"I knew your hardhead ass was gonna say dat."

When the sedans pull up, we both start cheesing from ear to ear. They are triple-black identical twins.

Ricky says, "Minez looks better den yours."

I darn near drive to Indianapolis going to get Chester. The car holds me hostage. I have never driven a vehicle that responds so quickly. When I pull up in front of Regina's I see Chester and Regina's mother in the back yard. Regina's mother has taken it upon herself to remove the yellow police tape. She's wrapped it all in a ball and is tossing it in the trash can. I see the soapy water running down the walkway. She must have cleared away everything. I guess she said later for waiting for the police to say it was okay.

Regina's mother is a lot more round than Regina. At first glance one would mistake her for a white woman. We seldom say more than three words to each other. She has never pretended to like me, and I don't pretend with her. Walking down the gangway, I see her pick up Chester and carry him in the house; they don't notice me.

At the back door I am about to knock, but something tells me to turn around. I do and get an unobstructed view of Mr. Nelson standing at his back gate. I wave and he just stares at me. I wave again, and still nothing. He's not moving, just standing there staring. Maybe he's gone back to drinking. I wouldn't blame him if he did. He beckons me with a couple of hand gestures. Damn it, I don't feel like talking to him right now.

Driving my new BMW, along with the prospect of

spending the evening with my son, has me feeling real nice. Getting back in the heavy mood of grieving is not on my agenda, but I walk to him regardless.

At his gate he grabs me by the shoulder leads me up his walkway. He doesn't say a word. We walks up his porch steps to the back door.

Then he directs me to "Stand here, Mr. Price, right in front of me."

I do as he asks.

"Now turn around and face your back door." I do it.

He gets up real close behind me and whispers in my ear "It ain't but a stone toss away . . . even if I was drunk I wouldn't have missed."

Damn. I hear him loud and clear . . . but I am neither the police, a priest nor a judge, so it's really not my business.

Without turning to look at him I say, "Mr. Nelson, my part in all this is over. Why are you telling me this?"

"Because, Mr. Price, I want you to know that in the end, old drunk Mr. Nelson took care of his family and handled his business."

Looking over to Regina's back door, he's right—it is nothing but a stone toss away. He could have knocked Randolph Peal in the head with a rock and hurt him. I never even considered Mr. Nelson as a suspect. When I turn to face him he is gone.

I am startled by his sudden disappearance, but that doesn't stop me from making my own rapid exit. I quickly get across the alley and up Regina's walk to her back door. When I look back at Mr. Nelson's porch, I see his back door slam shut.

*God bless him.*

This case is closed as far as I am concerned. I'm ready to hang out with my son.

While knocking on Regina's door, I hear "Hey, Daddy-Man!" Chester yells through the screen door.

"Hey, Chester Price!" I yell back at him. Regina's mother opens the door and my boy leaps into my arms, and at this moment, for a brother like me, all is right with the world.

## About the Author

Tony Lindsay was born and raised in Chicago which explains his love for the city that is captured in every novel. He currently lives with his wife and three daughters in northwest Indiana very close to the Chicagoland area. He was educated at the University of Illinois majoring in Psychology. Directly after college he worked extensively in the mental health profession counseling adolescents. Later he switched careers and went into advertising sales where he worked for local Chicago newspapers: N'DIGO and Sun Times. Today, Tony is working on writing his next novel while managing his property management company LFL Realty.

# NOW AVAILABLE FROM

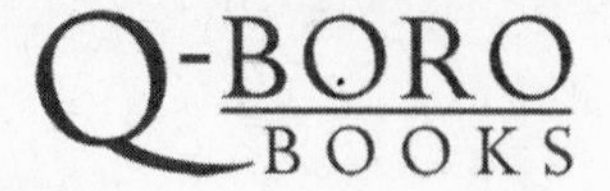

**NYMPHO**
**$14.95**
**ISBN 1933967102**

How will signing up to live a promiscuous double-life destroy everything that's at stake in the lives of two close couples? Take a journey into Leslie's secret world and prepare for a twisted, erotic experience.

**FREAK IN THE SHEETS**
**$14.95**
**ISBN 1933967196**

Ready to break out of the humdrum of their lives, Raquelle and Layla decide to put their knowledge of sexuality and business together and open up a freak school, teaching men and women how to please their lovers beyond belief while enjoying themselves in the process.
However, Raquelle and Layla must learn some important lessons when it comes to being a lady in the street and a freak in the sheets.

**LIAR, LIAR**
**$14.95**
**ISBN 1933967110**

Stormy calls off her wedding to Camden when she learns he's cheating with a male church member. However, after being convinced that Camden has been delivered from his demons, she proceeds with the wedding.
Will Stormy and Camden survive scandal, lies and deceit?

**HEAVEN SENT**
**$14.95**
**ISBN 1933967188**

Eve is a recovering drug addict who has no intentions of staying clean until she meets Reverend Washington, a newly widowed man with three children. Secrets are uncovered that threaten Eve's new life with her new family and has everyone asking if Eve was *Heaven Sent*.

**COMING SOON FROM**

# SEXXXfessions

*Confessions of an anonymous stripper*

**ANDREA BLACKSTONE**

AUTHOR OF NYMPHO

**FEBRUARY 2008**

**1-933967-31-5**

**COMING SOON FROM**

Q-BORO BOOKS

**FEBRUARY 2008**

1-933967-36-6

# COMING SOON FROM

# Q-BORO BOOKS

## MARCH 2008

1-933967-39-0